What the Critics are saying about:

Wanton Fire

PERFECT 10! "Quite possibly one of the most engrossing and riveting paranormals I've read this year, WANTON FIRE by Sherri L. King is a must read!" *~Courtney Bowden, Romance Reviews Today*

GOLD STAR! "I was not able to put it down until I finished. Wanton Fire is smoking hot! Full of danger, adventure, and suspense. I highly recommend that everyone run out and get this book for their home library." *~Susan Holly, Just Erotic Romance*

"...absolutely superb sequel to Ravenous. Again Sherri L. King excites us with her intriguing suspense and action packed scenes." *~Gail Northman, Romance Junkies*

Ravenous

PERFECT 10! "Hot enough to singe... one of the hottest paranormal books I've read this year. A must read for lovers of paranormal romances and erotica, RAVENOUS by Sherri L. King will slake any reader's desire!" *~Courtney Bowden, Romance Reviews Today*

5 STARS! "...quick, sexy and graphic! This is the kind of erotica every woman should relish in." *~Valerie Prince, Sime~gen*

5 STARS! "I absolutely could not put this book down! There was so much action and love and hot, wet, sizzling sex packed into this book...My compliments to Ms. King on such a breathtaking work." ~*Amy L. Turpin, Timeless Tales*

Mating Season

"A very enjoyable erotic read!"~*Sara Andrade, The Best Reviews*

"...a complete scorcher...Don't miss this keeper!"~*Sharyn McGinty, In the Library Reviews*

"A quick sizzling read...A delightful short story with tons of heat..."~Courtney Bowden, Romance Reviews Today

WANTON FIRE: THE HORDE WARS II
An Ellora's Cave Publication, October 2004

Ellora's Cave Publishing, Inc.
PO Box 787
Hudson, OH 44236-0787

ISBN #1419951149

This title has been previously published. The first edition is available in ebook form at www.ellorascave.com.

Cover art by Darrell King

Warning:

The following material contains graphic sexual content meant for mature readers. ***Wanton Fire: The Horde Wars II*** has been rated E–rotic by a minimum of three independent reviewers.

Ellora's Cave Publishing offers three levels of Romantica™ reading entertainment: S (S-ensuous), E (E-rotic), and X (X-treme).

S-e*nsuous* love scenes are explicit and leave nothing to the imagination.

E-*rotic* love scenes are explicit, leave nothing to the imagination, and are high in volume per the overall word count. In addition, some E-rated titles might contain fantasy material that some readers find objectionable, such as bondage, submission, same sex encounters, forced seductions, etc. E-rated titles are the most graphic titles we carry; it is common, for instance, for an author to use words such as "fucking", "cock", "pussy", etc., within their work of literature.

X-*treme* titles differ from E-rated titles only in plot premise and storyline execution. Unlike E-rated titles, stories designated with the letter X tend to contain controversial subject matter not for the faint of heart.

Wanton Fire
The Horde Wars II

By Sherri L. King

Some say the world will end in fire,
Some say in ice.
From what I've tasted of desire
I hold with those who favor fire.
But if it had to perish twice,
I think I know enough of hate
To say that for destruction ice
Is also great
And would suffice.

– *Robert Frost*

Prologue

They were surrounded by the Daemons; their entire group penned in by the monsters that were supposed to be too dull-witted to accomplish such a feat. But these Daemons…they were different from their predecessors. So very terrifyingly different. They seemed coordinated—a working unit with powers of strategic reasoning and logic—which was surely impossible. The beasts were mindless. They were vicious, evil and cruel to be sure, but mindless all the same, with no powers of higher reasoning. But this group, these seven creatures, had worked together against the three Shikar warriors, hemming them in back-to-back, facing outward against their foes.

The Shikars were tired, beyond exhaustion. For them it had already been a long night of hunting and killing these beasts among the jeopardized Territories of Earth. They'd saved the lives of countless humans this night, but they would not be able to save themselves. Not against these formidable foes. The warriors were breathless, gritting their teeth against the biting pain of their battle-worn muscles and bones, preparing themselves for a last stand against evil. It was all they could do. Their pride as warriors demanded that they stand their ground and face their deaths with courage and valor. They would not go down without putting up one hell of a fight.

The monsters stalked around them, as if judging the Shikars' strengths and how best to attack against them. Their burning yellow eyes were windows into hell's fire, gateways to the fiery pit itself, seeking—ever seeking—an opening to attack. An unspoken command seemed to pass between the vicious predators. In the next breath, as one, they rushed the Shikars, attacking en masse.

Shrieks of battle and death rang out into the night…then all fell silent.

Chapter One

Hamburg, Germany

"Would you quit that? You're embarrassing me! Just be cool, be real, and you'll blend right in."

"Cady, we've been blending in with humans since long before you were born," Obsidian growled. "We know what we're doing."

"Yeah. Right. Then if you're so damn comfortable out here why are you darting in between cars, ducking into corners, looking over your shoulder every few minutes, and basically appearing like you're a bunch of lunatic criminals? You're drawing far too much attention to us with your antics. *I've* noticed that you're not so great at subterfuge…and so has half of the city!"

"How would you have us act, Cady? Would you have us stand in the middle of the road and wait for an attack from any quarter? Is that what you would prefer?"

"You are such a jerk, Sid. Just be cool, as I said, and follow my lead." Cady sniffed the night air. "Ah ha. Hang on. I'll be right back." She darted across the dirty wet street and ducked into a garishly lit shop on the other side, leaving her group to stand behind and wait for her.

"I don't feel comfortable being out here like this, Obsidian." Edge's smooth voice betrayed none of his nervousness, despite his words to the contrary.

"Neither do I. But Cady thinks we'll find something here. We'll just have to bear with her until she knows more."

"I hate the stink of this place." Cinder scowled. "I much prefer the farmlands we've been frequenting of late. The smell of animals and crops is not so unnatural as…this." He gestured to the passing cars, wandering people, fast food restaurants and nightclubs that lined the dingy city street.

"Do you think I enjoy this any better than either of you? I would much rather be at home playing with my son or loving my woman until she bears me another. But we have a duty here and I'll be damned if we'll go back home before we kill a few Daemons this night." Obsidian looked around with no small amount of discomfort at their surroundings. Cady may be used to frequenting the world of humans—she was a former human after all—but he definitely was not. Where Edge and Cinder often frequented the surface world to find willing female companionship, he himself had not often found the time to so indulge himself before meeting Cady, his wife. He was ill at ease here, on the surface world.

He thought back to the meeting between himself and his love…if so tame a word as 'meeting' could be used to describe the cataclysmic effect they'd had upon each other that first night. They'd fought like wildcats, each sustaining injuries from the other, battling for supremacy in those first few moments of confrontation with a tireless fervor. They still warred for supremacy of each other, fighting for the upper hand in almost every situation, no matter how insignificant. Though now instead of ending their skirmishes with bloodshed and bruises they usually ended up settling things in bed.

Obsidian smiled dangerously. He often enjoyed pricking his mate's temper if only to spice up the play in their bed. She was a fiery lover. More than a match for his voracious Shikar appetites. Sex with her was explosive and truly amazing…when it wasn't mind-blowing, tender, full of gentle kisses and soft-spoken vows of love. He would never tire of her. And he would see to it that she never tired of him.

He loved her more than life itself.

And now he had a son, Armand—named after Cady's lost baby brother, the tragic victim of a Daemon attack—thus his heart was full of tender emotions. His son was the image of himself, with his mother's impish smile and mischievous ways. He was perfect. Never in his life had Obsidian expected to be so blessed in so short a time. But now he was a husband and a father…and more than ever he vowed to defeat the threat that could one day snatch those precious things away from him. Cady and Armand were his life. He would protect them with all of his being and more.

Cady emerged from the shop with a sack in her hand. She came to their sides with a slightly smug, yet gamin grin on her face, drawing Obsidian from his inner musings.

"Ta da! Now these will help us appear more like tourists instead of no-good thugs. Ever had a foot-long with the works?"

Cinder laughed. "I always have a foot-long that works."

"Ha, ha. You are such a geek, Cin. I mean a foot-long hot dog—bratwurst actually, I think." She pulled out a cylindrical package of foil and handed it to him. "Try it, you'll like it. It's loads better than your usual Shikar-grown mutton or grain, if you ask me. Ugh. I am getting so tired of eating the same old stuff day in and day out. Maybe Tryton will be willing to import some fast food now and then if I ask." She distributed her treasures to Edge and Obsidian, keeping one for herself, then showed them how best to open and eat the confections without getting the messy toppings all over themselves.

Hot dogs? Cinder looked at Edge and sent him a worried, questioning look. Were they really expected to eat *dog*? Edge shrugged, looking as confused as he felt. Cinder sniffed the food and winced. It smelled tangy and rancid and he was certain that the clear, white topping upon it was inedible. "What is this?" he asked, picking up a piece of the warm, squishy stuff.

"Sauerkraut. It's fermented cabbage. Try it," she said firmly, "you'll like it." Cady took a healthy bite of hers and Cinder struggled not to turn green.

Fermented cabbage? In other words, it was rotten. He'd be damned before he ate anything *rotten*. Cinder smiled and, to please Cady, he took a tiny bite out of the end of his poor, cooked dog. The dog tasted far worse than it smelled! He quickly turned his head away from the others and spat the offensive refuse out onto the street. He held the hot dog behind his back, focused his energy, and burned it to a crisp in his hand. He crumpled the ashes and let them scatter harmlessly on the wind behind him.

Edge sent him an angry look. He would not get off the hook so easily as Cinder had. He had not the skill of an Incinerator. Edge was on his own. Cinder sent him a smug grin and dusted his hands clean of the offensive food.

"You're already finished, Cin? Good grief, you must have been hungry—why didn't you say something earlier?

Here, have another." Cady reached into the paper sack and retrieved another of the awful dogs. Cinder tried not to cringe. "See? I told you they were good." She smiled, but Cinder could have sworn that she knew—somehow actually knew—what he had done with the first dog.

Cinder bit back a groan and accepted another foot-long from Cady's hand. Edge chuckled and took a daring bite out of his own…Cinder was surprised when he took yet another, larger bite, after that. Edge was obviously possessed of a much higher tolerance than he for the horrible human food.

"What exactly are we looking for here, Cady?"

"What are we always looking for, Cin? Daemons."

"But here, in the middle of a city? Of all the places they've frequented of late, I haven't heard a tale involving such a populated place."

"And why do you think that is? Any clues? I've often wondered myself why these creatures don't just swarm into a city and take their pick of the humans that wander about here," Cady pressed.

"Maybe psychics only frequent unpopulated areas," supplied Edge, who still munched contentedly on his hot dog.

"Again—why? Don't you ever wonder about these things?"

"No doubt, even as dull-witted as Daemons are, they know better than to tempt fate and discovery by entering large cities." Obsidian sighed, clearly impatient. "But we are not here to question their ways, and to do so will only waste precious time. We are here to protect…and I don't see anyone who needs protecting right this moment."

"Trust me, Sid. I have a feeling. We need to be here tonight. I can just feel it, okay?"

Obisdian sighed and pulled her tight against his side. "We'll stay close to one another and stay aware. You'll let us know when you sense any changes around us, if I don't sense them first." He winked at his wife. They were always in competition with each other now to see who had the strongest Hunter skills. "But I don't like being in so crowded a place. I don't like thinking that a Daemon would dare come here and wreak havoc. I don't like it at all."

"Neither do I," Cady agreed.

The group was silent for several long moments as the human world moved on in ignorance around them. Cinder quickly burned his second bratwurst and scanned the people that littered the streets. Such an odd group, humans. He had little use for them, really. Neither did any of the other Shikars to his knowledge. He only really interacted with them when he needed a woman…or two. He did so love human women. Their soft arms, plump thighs, tender hearts and welcoming bodies were the stuff of decadent dreams. He would have preferred that the human race run itself into extinction as it seemed so wont to do but for the loss of the women.

Cinder was drawn out of his thoughts as Cady went still. Something was amiss.

Cady's breath misted into the air as she exhaled a long, pent up breath. She leaned into the night, swaying out of Obsidian's arms, eyes going heavy and distant. Cinder watched the process with a growing alarm. Cady's strength as a Shikar Warrior of the Hunter and Incinerator Castes grew by leaps and bounds every day. It never ceased to amaze him how powerful she had become…was becoming. He tried to remember what life had been like before she had joined their ranks. She had been a human woman then. She had been an amazing warrior even then. But now…she was the stuff of legends.

"Holy Horde, they're close." Her voice was hoarse, strained.

"How close? How many?" Obsidian demanded.

"I don't know." Her voice broke. "They feel so different. Their presence seems so strong one moment and then just…it just kind of fades away.

"How can that be?" Edge asked.

Cady ignored him. "C'mon. There's something this way."

"How many are there, damn it?"

"I don't know, Sid!" Cady's arms flailed in frustration and her long braid whipped about her shoulders and back. "I'm not even certain what I'm feeling is the presence of a Daemon or something else. But whatever it is, it's strong, and it's this way. So just follow me, all right?"

"On your guard everyone," Obsidian cautioned.

He didn't have to warn them twice. Cinder felt the fire that was always burning just beneath his flesh, begin to kindle and spark. He didn't like this situation. None of them did. But he would see that these humans were kept safe from whatever threat was posed to them, if that was the will of The Elder, Tryton—and it was.

Lately Tryton seemed quite obsessed with humans.

The four of them moved efficiently through the crowded sidewalks until they came upon a thundering nightclub.

"The Desolate?" Edge said, easily translating the German sign that hung above the establishment, the words blinking in bright neon colors that belied the darkness of the name. "Sounds quaint."

"It's an industrial or techno club, I think." Cady looked the place over with a thorough attention to detail.

"What the hell does that mean?" Obsidian asked.

"Industrial and techno are types of music. Very loud, very heavy music with complex beats and such. That's all I know. I was a fan of very few bands in my youth—I didn't really have much time for music."

"Would you look at these humans?" Edge muttered in their Shikar tongue so as not to offend the natives. "They look so somber with their white faces and funeral garb."

"Not all of them." Cinder tried not to gawk when he saw a woman sporting a two-foot high Mohawk in various colors and shades of the rainbow. Her piercing struck Cinder as particularly interesting. She had rings and bars in her ears, eyebrows, nose, lips…she even sported silver studs lined in a row up each alabaster forearm. He'd never seen their like before. She wore a clear plastic top with red dots positioned just over her nipples, and a long red velvet skirt. "Wow," Cinder breathed, unable to tear his eyes off of the spectacle.

"Well. Let's go in."

"Wait. You can't be serious, baby, surely."

"I don't want to go in there any more than you do, Sid. But we have to…that's all there is to it."

Cady produced a thick wad of human currency—Tryton kept them well supplied for their ventures above the surface, though how he obtained the funds was a mystery and probably better left as such—and paid their entrance fees. Cinder walked in ahead of the group, curious about what lay in wait for them in this strange place. They passed through a door into a dimly lit foyer. There, a shirtless man in black latex pants asked them for proof of ID. Cady produced their documents—high quality forgeries procured through Tryton—for the man to view, and they were admitted through yet another door.

Here was a place of thundering, shadowy chaos. Blinding white strobe lights pulsed about them in the dark, revealing in flashes a huge group of undulating human bodies. The Shikars were on the outskirts of a dance floor, swallowed by the throng of people that pumped and swayed to the heady music. Cinder winced. The air was thick as syrup with the noise. It pulled at him like a weight, and every bass-ridden beat of the music thudded in his chest with the force of a physical blow.

"This isn't so bad." Cady yelled to be heard over the din.

"Are you mad? This is horrendous. It reminds me of the Gates…except the air is easier to breathe," Edge yelled back.

"I expected much worse. The DJ is pretty good."

"What the hell are you talking about?" Edge was growing more and more agitated as the music swarmed around them like the thunder of the Horde's giant heartbeats.

"DJ—disc jockey. I wonder who it is?"

"I give up. You've lost me entirely—but I don't care. I can't stay here. The noise, the crowd, the lights…it's all too much. What, by Grimm, are we supposed to find here?"

"I don't know." Cady had the gall to laugh when Edge glowered at her. Cady never lacked for gall.

Cinder looked around them. The place was swarming with humans. It was such a wild and busy place, this nightclub. He'd never witnessed its equal in chaos and celebration…for that seemed what the humans were intent on doing. Celebrating. They drank heavy spirits, kissed and fondled in a sea of damp, tender limbs, and danced in rhythm with the music. He saw them all as they probably would have least liked to appear. Fragile, vulnerable creatures who were not long for the world they so took for granted. A small woman bumped into him, then turned and rubbed her soft, plump body against his. He took her in his arms and undulated back against her, marveling that so small and luscious a creature could approach one as dangerous as he without a care for her own safety.

"Don't stray too far, Cinder." He heard Obsidian call out behind him but was more riveted by the sea of bodies that moved to swallow him up. His partner rose up, pressing her scantily clad body even more firmly against him, and kissed him full on the lips.

Cinder tasted alcohol and amphetamines on her breath, but he kissed her anyway. Her lush, precious mortality clouded over him like a thick perfume. Their kiss ended and Cinder clearly saw in her eyes the invitation for more serious play. But he set her back with a gentle smile and used his preternatural speed to escape without her notice. He was sure she was too inebriated to notice his seeming disappearance. He let the crowd take him deep.

The music had changed tempo but he couldn't remember when. Now it was not so fast as it was thick and plaintive a tune. The lights flashed so that he could find no peace from their invasion, even when he closed his eyes. Men and women alike rubbed against him in a brutal, sexual dance that had his senses reeling. He'd never felt so out of control, so in tune with a chaos that beckoned with the promise of fleshly love and lust even as it bludgeoned him into madness and confusion. Time lost all meaning. The music played on and he was forced to worship it, along with everyone else.

Cinder gasped for breath that did not have the salty-sweet taste of human sweat. He could catch no sight of his group in the flashing confusion, and upon realizing just how long he'd been immersed in this pagan dance, he searched for a way to the edge of the dance floor. He finally broke free and had a moment to look around, to collect himself and his drunken senses.

A flash of pink hair caught his eye and held it riveted. The vibrant hair belonged to a woman, young in form and face. A lovely woman. Cinder could see, even from this distance that she was heavily painted, heavily submerged in the role—whatever it was—best suited to the atmosphere of this strange place.

Her lips were glistening, glittering red, a full and delicious looking mouth. Her large hazel eyes were rimmed in thick black lines, her lashes dripping with similar cosmetic adornment. She wore a tight outfit—a shiny second skin of some strange man-made material—consisting of a sleeveless top, which also left her toned abdomen exposed, pants that rode low on her boyishly slim hips, and chunky-heeled, thigh-high boots. Of all the people in the club, she looked as though the clothes had been made especially for her. She wore them with a negligent style that drew the eye and held it...at least in his case.

She stood on a dais or stage of sorts, bathed in a halo of blue and red lights. She wore a strange headset at her ear as she moved in time to the music. Her lusciously kissable lips were pursed in concentration as she studied the table before her, and the discs that spun upon it. Cinder instinctively guessed that the music mercilessly pounding through the place played forth at her orchestration. She was responsible for the otherworldly tempos stealing through him like a thief in search of his soul.

He couldn't pull his gaze away from her. There was just something indefinable about her, setting her apart from the humans gathered around at her feet. She seemed some kind of pagan goddess as the crowd raised supplicant arms to her, begging her for more, crying out for the music to keep flowing. He'd never seen anything like it in all of his many years as a warrior. He'd never seen anything like *her*.

He stood there for…he couldn't have guessed how long. Minutes? Hours? He didn't—couldn't care. He watched the ethereal goddess orchestrate her music, dance to her music, count out the beats of her music as she changed seamlessly from one song to the next. A singular eternity could have passed and he wouldn't have worried about it, so long as he could watch her.

A green-haired man stepped up from the crowd, moved to her and whispered in her ear. Cinder felt an inconsolable sense of jealousy and loss. The man was too familiar with her. He knew her intimately; he had to for taking such liberties as kissing her on one of her alluringly bared shoulders. He had no right to feel such things for the woman, was foolish to even come close to such a passion for a human. But there it was—he was weak where she was concerned, in a way he'd never been weak before. He wanted to turn away, wanted to leave this crazy place that was filled with temptation and want and need.

But just as he turned, just as he found the strength to walk away from the siren behind the turntable, the music changed. The woman stepped back from her post and flexed her shoulders as if they ached. Pink and black waves of hair danced about her as she jauntily descended down from the stage and disappeared into the throng of people, leaving Cinder to take in the seemingly endless length of her legs as she walked. His heart thundered.

He especially favored women with long limbs…and she had the longest legs he'd ever seen.

A voice sounded over the loudspeaker as the music boomed loud enough to wake the entire Horde. "Let's hear it for our own, incomparable DJ SteffyStealth!" The announcement was voiced in thick German words.

Cinder waited a moment, fighting his impulses, which had become irrationally fixated on the woman…and then followed her through the crowd.

Chapter Two

The flashing lights from the strobes overhead hypnotized Steffy. The primitive, rhythmic beats of the music pounded through her veins like sweet honey, lulling her. She became the music. Was one with it as she spun the records on her turntable, counting out the beats in her head with effortless ease and skill. She felt elemental, powerful and alive. In control of herself and the world around her. Behind the turntable, surrounded by her sound equipment, was the only time she ever felt truly free of worry or stress.

It was the only time she felt relaxed.

She undulated with the music, counted off the beats that resounded in the headset she wore on one ear and switched the records, never missing tempo so that the tunes were artfully mixed into one ongoing, endless song. The crowd thundered its approval with the stomping of feet as they danced and moved, one with the music that pounded through the club's massive sound system. Steffy looked out over her deck and felt a heady thrill upon seeing the massive crowd sway like one giant serpentine body under the lights. In perfect accord with her musical rhythm.

Steffy saw the club's entertainment coordinator saunter up next to her on the stage and sent him a brilliant smile. The man was truly delicious, dressed in his shining, black bondage wear, with his short green hair spiked up artfully on top of his head. It was a good thing for her libido that Dika was a firm homosexual or she'd be drooling as he drew closer to her.

"You've been going at it for three hours, Steffy, love. Why not take a break?" he asked in thickly accented German, yelling his words into her ear in order to be heard over the din.

"Just let me spin this next track out and I'll take fifteen," she yelled back.

"You've blown us away tonight, love. I haven't seen this large a crowd here since…well, never." He laughed. "You're making a huge name for yourself, my dear. And to think a year ago you simply waltzed in off the street and demanded a job, with no prior experience. I'm so glad I threw caution to the wind and gave you a chance. Best decision I ever made!"

"Don't you forget it." She counted the beats in her mind, keeping part of her attention on Dika's words and another part—the most important part—on the music. A thick, disheveled lock of neon pink hair fell into her left eye but she was too intent on other things to blow it out of her line of sight. "Now leave me alone so I can finish this session," she quipped.

Dika leaned over and, as was his way, pressed a flirtatious but totally meaningless kiss to her bare shoulder before winking and trotting off, swaying his rear with the grace of a runway model as he went. A few minutes later her set came to an end and she smoothly switched the play from the spinning record to the CD player below the table. As Rammstein's *Bestrafe Mich* played from the sound system, she left her position behind the turntable deck and made her way through the crowd, towards the bar.

"Let's hear it for our own, incomparable DJ SteffyStealth!" Dika's voice announced her stage name over the speaker system and thunderous applause was the result, as well as congratulations and compliments from many of the people around her.

God, she was tired.

This weariness had been growing in her for the past year—she couldn't escape it. Only the music had the power to distance her from the desolation that threatened to take her under. The fire of life that had always burned so brightly within her was diminished. It had been dwindling ever since she'd returned from her stint as a foreign exchange student in the United States. She needed quickening—some inspiration and excitement—and she needed it soon or else she would lose herself to this despair.

Boredom had always been her greatest enemy.

She thought about boredom. How it had gotten her into all of the trouble she'd ever been in over the years—and that had been plenty enough. It was what had made her drunkard father beat her into submission during the first fifteen years of her life, the bastard. Boredom was what had made her finish her schooling early—the year of her fifteenth birthday—only to take to the streets during the lonely, uneventful days that had followed her graduation and flight from home. It was what had made her such a good car thief for the next couple of years—causing her to seek out the thrill and danger of the life of a delinquent. It was what had made her leave that life behind, after she'd become the best at her craft—such as it was—to enroll in college and subsequently to participate in an exchange program.

Where she had met Raine.

Steffy pushed these thoughts from her mind. Better to suffer the boredom than the pain that lay down that road of memories.

"I liked your music very much."

Steffy started and turned to face the owner of the purring voice. That she could hear him over the sound system proved how close he'd gotten to her without her noticing—no mean feat with her heightened senses. He was right on top of her. In the cannon shots of the strobe light she caught sight of a tall, broad shouldered, platinum-haired man. He was dressed—surprise, surprise—in clinging black garb from his thick neck down to his large booted feet.

"*Danke*." She thanked him and turned away.

"It is chaos and darkness. I've never heard the like before."

So he was one of *those* people, having to see some meaning and underlying passion in music that she, essentially, threw out on a whim. She liked the music, loved to spin it out, but beyond that it had no real meaning. At least, she didn't like to think so. It was only math, really. Rhythms and patterns and numbers in her head.

"Thanks," she said again and made her way to the bar. "Vodka—straight," she requested from the bartender. She tapped out the rhythm of the music on the surface of the bar with her black painted nails.

"My name is Cinder."

Cinder? She laughed. "Taking the hardcore Goth image a little far aren't we?"

"What do you mean?" He seemed genuinely puzzled.

Steffy shook her head with a sarcastic chuckle, took a seat upon one of the bar stools, and accepted her drink. She braced herself and tipped the clear, fiery liquid down her throat. It took all of her concentration not to gasp or cough, but she managed. Within seconds she was feeling a little better—the endless cold of her bones subsiding in the warmth of the drink—and she was a little less cranky towards the man who took an uninvited seat next to her.

"What do you mean?" He repeated his question.

"Nothing. Is Cinder your real name, then?" She sighed with resignation, realizing the man would not leave any time soon.

"Yes. My father gave it to me upon the eve of my birth. He sensed in me my ability to w—" He trailed off, looking a little discomfited. "I'm sorry. The noise of this place has me a little off balance."

"No shit."

"What is your name?"

Steffy could see the burn of desire in his eyes. The flame burst of his orange-yellow contact lenses only added to the effect and she shuddered. Instinctively she knew that this man was a danger. She rose from her seat and walked back into the crowd, seeking escape in the camouflage of the masses.

His hand nearly scorched her flesh when he caught her arm.

"I have offended you? I am sorry."

Steffy gritted her teeth. She hated his familiarity, his strength, which was easy enough for her to sense with or without the aid of her uncanny intuition. "Leave me be," she said softly, dangerously, locking her eyes to his.

The man's face hardened and grew shadowed beneath the flashing lights. "You are very rude. I don't know why I expected more of you."

"I don't either. So buzz off." She used Raine's favorite slang phrase. Americans had a slang phrase for every occasion, it seemed.

The man crowded against her, the heat baking off of his body nearly suffocating her. He moved with the ebb and flow of the people that surrounded them, taking her easily into a dance that she had no desire to join in. His eyes burned down into hers, intimidating and predatory, and for a moment she felt her courage falter. She sensed something in him that could frighten her if she let it.

She wouldn't.

"If you don't let me pass this instant, I will call security and have you thrown out."

"Try it."

She felt her eyes grow wide with the force of her shock. "Are you threatening me?"

"No. I am daring you. Call your security. Let's see what happens."

"Are you some kind of mental case or something?"

"All I want is your name."

"You *are* a mental case."

His hand tightened on her arm, pulling her closer to him. He was tall. Very tall. She was tall for a woman at five foot eight, but he towered over her despite her own stature. It was not a little discomfiting, to be so shadowed by him at this close range. She took in his features, which were exotic and unique. He appeared savage and decidedly foreign in some indefinable way that had her studying him more closely out of sheer, mesmerized curiosity.

He was unlike any other man she'd ever seen, the sum total of his appearance seeming alien to her stunned senses. His cheekbones and nose were honed blades beneath smooth golden skin. His mouth was almost cruel in its sensuality. His chin was hard and strong. Incredibly stubborn. Again came the sense that he was dangerous.

Far too dangerous for her to underestimate.

"Your name," he bit out.

"You'll get nothing from my name, ass. Everyone in this place knows me. If you try anything, you'll regret it."

"Why is it so hard to give me your name? Will your green-haired man become jealous if you share it with me?"

"Green-haired man? You mean Dika?" She laughed. "Dika's just a friend. Besides, he's gay." What had possessed her to admit that much to him? She couldn't have said.

His eyes burned with something close to triumph as Steffy bitterly regretted giving him so much information. His teeth blazed white with his smile. "Well, if everyone knows you here, then I could get your name from them with much less trouble. But I'd rather hear it from you. And with your stubborn refusal to share it, you have made it a challenge. I've never been able to resist a challenge."

Steffy felt her arm burn beneath his hand.

"Your name. Please." He softened his tone and his hold. The heat of his touch ebbed.

"Stefany Michanke. I am the DJ here. People will miss me if I am gone," she warned him with a diamond-hard look.

"Stefany, was that so very hard?" His lips twisted in a small smile. He leaned into her, swaying against her slowly, sexily. He inhaled a long breath. "You smell great."

Okay. He was getting way too forward for her liking. She wrested herself from his hold and prepared to flee but something—someone—caught her eye before she could make good her escape.

A black-haired man, taller and broader than Cinder, had appeared at their side. Her senses must be failing her tonight—she'd never been taken by surprise like this before, twice in one night. Maybe it was the vodka…but Cinder had come upon her in stealth before she'd drunk it.

"Cinder, come at once."

And as quickly as that he was gone. If Steffy had blinked she would have missed the two men walking away, towering over the people in the crowd, somehow set apart from all the rest not only by their height but by their grace and bearing. Wherever they were going they were headed there with deadly intent.

Steffy watched as they left the club. They were so different from the people who surrounded them. Something about the way they held themselves, the way they walked and spoke…it puzzled her. Intrigued her. She hadn't failed to notice that their eyes took in the surroundings as if they were scoping out the place, reassuring themselves of the advantages or disadvantages of their positions within it. She would have bet her every last CD that the men knew exactly where all the entrances and exits were located. That they knew where every member of security was stationed.

They were dangerous, these two, she could *feel* it.

She gritted her teeth against a sudden, inexplicably foolish urge. She tried to ignore this urge…but it was hopeless. She waited several minutes, warring with herself, knowing what she was about to do was probably pretty stupid. She couldn't help it. She had to do it.

Boredom had fled. Her interest was piqued. Where before she would have left Cinder standing alone on the floor—quite content to never see the guy again—she was now ready to pursue him. Doggedly. She wanted to know where he was going. Signaling to Dika that she was leaving for the night, she made her way through the maze of people. Senses keen and at the ready, she followed in the direction the two men had taken.

* * * * *

Steffy walked down a few winding back alleys, sensing more than really knowing what direction they had chosen. Before long, she approached what she knew to be an abandoned lot, mostly overgrown now with an old, dilapidated petrol station rotting down in the middle of it. From the shadowy lot came sounds she instantly understood and recognized—shouts, groans, and the thudding sound of flesh against flesh. Being a former delinquent herself, she was no stranger to the unmistakable cacophony of a knockdown, drag out fight.

She wondered idly if the two men were in some sort of gang together.

Probably. They had looked dangerous enough, that was for sure, even if they did look a little too well bred for such pursuits. They looked more like wild CIA rejects, actually, than gang members.

A flash of fire illuminated the night.

Steffy shrieked softly in surprise.

A body streaked out of the darkness that followed, taking her to the ground with a jarring thud.

"Who the fuck are you?" came the savage, female voice. Heat baked from the woman, nearly scalding Steffy's skin.

Steffy bucked, sending her attacker rolling. She gained her feet and pursued, but the darkness shrouded her enemy in secrecy. A click sounded at her ear—the cocking of a pistol—and she froze. The woman had managed to creep up behind her in the dark. Amazing considering her keen senses, even in this blackness.

"Jesus! How'd you get here, DJ girl?"

The sounds of battle were louder, more chaotic now about them. The music that always played in Steffy's head rose to a crescendo in rhythm with it and she gritted her teeth, losing herself a little to the adrenaline that surged within her veins. "I followed Cinder, genius."

Laughter grated out from the fearsome voice. "I like you already. Here. Take this. And for God's sake, stay out of sight."

A thick handgun was shoved inelegantly into her hands.

"Do you know how to use that?" the voice asked impatiently.

Another fireball lit the night, illuminating the woman's features. Bright orange-yellow eyes burned at Steffy from a beautiful, proud face. The warrior woman looked more like a sex kitten in her ebony cat suit than a gang member. The moment took on a surrealism that almost made her laugh.

"Yeah, sure, I know how to use it. You just point and shoot." What self-respecting ex-streeter didn't know how to use a gun?

"Good." The woman grinned. Her dangerous demeanor was lessened, making her look younger, prettier. "Now stay behind this wall." Steffy looked around and only then noticed that she was behind one of the crumbling walls of the old petrol station. The woman continued, words clipped and matter of fact. "If anything icky comes out at you, you fire this gun until it's empty and you call for help. Okay?"

The woman had lapsed from flawless German into equally flawless English. Luckily, Steffy was fluent and understood her words. "Okay," she answered in kind. "Sure." The situation seemed more than a little absurdly overdramatic and she was at a loss for anything beyond her soft reply.

In a flash the woman was gone.

The ground thudded as the battle beyond the wall continued. There came a savage, inhuman scream, and then the roar of flame. The swift staccato of machine gun fire echoed…the music in Steffy's head changed tempo, gaining in speed and urgency.

What the hell was going on?

Her skin crawled. The hairs on her arms and nape stood on end. She tightened her fingers on the grip of the gun in her hand. Something was close, something dangerous and threatening. Every instinct screamed at her not to do it...but curiosity got the better of her and she peeked out from behind her hiding place.

"*Scheiße*!" She shrieked and pulled back behind the wall, gasping, heart racing.

Her mind would not, could not, process the image she had just seen to anything that was understandable or believable. Heaven help her but she had to take a second look. If only to reassure herself that the...*thing*...was not there. That she had somehow imagined it.

Trembling she peeked out again. Her eyes met and held with bloodshot, orange orbs. "Holy hell," she moaned and fell back behind the wall once more.

Had it seen her in the darkness? It was several feet away and she was cloaked in shadow...maybe it hadn't seen her. She was suddenly, sickeningly sure that it had. Her stomach rolled and she gagged. The smell of brimstone and old death assailed her sensitive nostrils and she doubled over, emptying the contents of her stomach in a heated rush onto the ground.

What hideous abomination had been let loose from its prison in hell tonight? That was no fairy tale monster she had glimpsed—no imagination under God could have spawned such a savage vision as that, surely. That was a devil or a demon or a monster. There was no adequate word in any language for what that thing was.

A growl purred at her ear. She took a deep breath, steeling herself instinctively to face the mortal danger she knew she had to confront. Reality had checked itself out of her consciousness the moment she had met Cinder. Now was the time for action, not rationality. Another growl sounded...and the wall above her head exploded.

"*Scheiße*!" she screamed again and leaped back, raising the gun before her as she retreated in horror.

She looked into the face of pure evil…and knew that her life would never again be the same.

Hesitating no longer she fired, point blank, into the tusked mouth of the creature. Thick black ooze, like tar or glue, flew out in a spray, hot and gooey down her front as the monster's face exploded. Steffy gasped and leapt further back. Her hand shook on the gun and her vision grayed. Thick, pounding music played on in her mind—her own personal soundtrack that never seemed to fall quiet—and her heartbeat matched its violently raging tempo.

Then…her heart almost stopped beating. Adrenaline took over and she would have fallen if not for its bracing strength. The monster gasped, spraying black muck once more with the bellow of its breath…and advanced on her.

"For fuck's sake!" She fired the gun into its gaping maw once again.

It faltered. It choked on a growl. It righted itself. And continued to advance.

Steffy screamed in rage and fear and emptied the gun into the monster's torn and oozing head. And still the creature came for her. The gun was empty, the clip devoid of any more bullets. The creature reached out for her and she beat its clawed hands back with the gun, clubbing it over and over again. And still it came.

"Help!" she yelled, and turning, she fled from the creature as she had never fled from anything in her life. "Help me, damn it!"

She had no idea in which direction to run. Her mind was a quandary of confusion, fear, and desperation. How could anything live after taking so many shots full on in the face? How would she ever be able to sleep comfortably again knowing that these things existed? Her world was chaos, her terror absolute.

Fire lit the night, illuminating her way…as she fled directly into the path of yet another creature.

She stopped so fast that she slid forward, then lost balance and fell back onto her tailbone. Her hands saved her from a terrible bruising but only just. The crumbling asphalt beneath her cut and scraped her palms bloody and the pain thankfully served to sharpen her senses to a knife's honed edge. She scrambled backwards, crablike, and desperately tried to regain her feet.

The creature before her roared and the sound of it echoed in her mind, mixing into the music. The monster was upon her. She had nowhere to go. She was unarmed.

She was going to die.

Gritting her teeth, she steeled herself. No way would she die with a scream on her lips. If this was to be her end, she would face it with as much courage as she could. She would not leave this world without injuring her killer first…somehow.

A shadow passed before her. A wind, like the cool breath of a gentle death, played in her hair, streaking it across her eyes so that it blinded her. She shook the locks away, blinked her blurry eyes, and gasped at the scene that unfolded before her.

A black-cloaked man moved calmly, gracefully to intercept her attacker, standing almost upon her, as if she wasn't even there. He slowly extended his hand out before him, as if he were moving in the thick fog of a dream. His palm splayed, landing gently upon the chest of the beast as it charged them. The man disappeared. The monster faltered, then fell, and Steffy only just managed to move aside as it came crashing to the ground right where she had been but a moment before. The man appeared once more, behind the fallen creature, as calm and collected as he had been during the entire confrontation. Looking down upon her from his hooded visage, he stood still as a statue. As still as death.

Steffy choked on a cry, whether of terror or awe she couldn't have said.

Long black cloth danced about his form on a wind that wasn't there. The man's hand was still held out before him, only now it held a giant pulsating orb. The monster's heart. Steffy knew instinctively that this was the monster's heart. Somehow, without breaching the wall of the creature's chest, the man had taken its heart and with it the life that beat within it.

"Cinder." The man's voice was like the ringing of hell's bells. Deadly, frightening…yet indescribably beautiful. Alluring, it could tempt any man or woman to sell their soul without a qualm. The man tossed the heart over her head and, in a daze, she looked back to see Cinder catch it in his hand. It burnt to ash within the next breath, though Steffy hadn't seen him set a match or lighter to it.

The cloaked man whirled then as yet another monster came up behind him, and within the blink of an eye he had taken that creature's heart in a similar fashion as he had the first. How he performed such a trick she couldn't have guessed. But the night was full of magic, evil and good or so it would seem, and it didn't seem to matter that none of it made any logical sense.

Steffy tried twice before she found a voice with which to speak. "Thank you," she said to the cloaked man. She rose, turned about, and extended the thanks to Cinder then and was shocked when he came forward and pushed her roughly into the arms of the other.

"Get her out of here, Traveler," he growled.

"And where shall I take her?" came the sardonic question above her as the cloaked man steadied her against him with strong, firm hands.

"The fuck out of here," came the voice of the woman as she rushed past them at a dead run. "We've got more coming!"

Cinder sent her a burning look then nodded to the man who held her. "Get her to safety. We'll deal with what she's seen later."

He followed in the wake of the woman, leaving Steffy alone with the quiet, hooded one.

"What the hell is going on here? What are these things?" She tried to pull away from the steely hard body that dwarfed her.

Her vision grew dim, the world dissolved around her, and when it righted itself again it no longer seemed any world with which she was familiar. The petrol station was gone. She was standing in a dimly lit chamber of iron and stone.

"Wait here," said the beautiful voice from the shadowy cowl. And the man disappeared, leaving her there.

"*Scheiße,*" she breathed and fell to her knees on the stone floor, shaking.

No doubt about it. Boredom was indeed the most dangerous force that drove her life.

Chapter Three

Steffy had looked the odd apartment over twice and it seemed the only way out was through a massive iron door, which was locked tight, trapping her within. She had studied the door, thinking and pondering her predicament, and there was really only one choice open to her. The lock was an old, antique design. The kind one might expect to see in an old church or dilapidated homestead.

It would be child's play for her to pick it.

Steffy bent down and pulled off her shiny black boot. Strapped to her ankle beneath it was a small lock picking kit, her constant companion ever since her days as a petty thief. Not that she'd had much use for it in recent years. Except for the time she and her friend Raine had stolen into one of the dormitories and rigged the PA system to play a Ministry CD at ear-splitting volume. Steffy pushed the memory away before it had time to bloom…she missed her friend too much to remember her without pain. And she had no time for weakness now. She removed the kit from her ankle and laid it out on the floor before the door.

She took a deep breath. And let her instincts take over.

Less than sixty seconds later the door was unlocked and she was putting her boot back on over the lock picks, strapped once more to her ankle.

"Still got the moves, heaven help me," she muttered to herself.

The door was cold against her hands as she cautiously eased it open a crack, just enough for her to see if the coast was clear. Thankfully it was. She opened the door wider and quickly ducked her head out into the passageway beyond it for a better look around. The light was dim in the corridor, but bright enough for her to see her way around with relative ease.

It seemed then that the room behind her was a safer haven than whatever lay beyond the door. She hadn't a clue where she was, except for an innate sense that she just might be deep underground, and it made her nervous. Unsure of herself now, she had to force that first step away from the stone and iron room. Luckily, each subsequent step was easier until she was silently gliding with swift ease down the shadowy corridors leading away from her prison.

Her eyes darted about warily, searching for any dangers or threats that might otherwise lay hidden. There were none. The passageway was empty before her, stretching on until blackness swallowed its progress far beyond.

What kind of place was this, that the ceilings were so high the dim light could barely reach to illuminate them? That every surrounding surface was carved of solid rock, at times plain and unadorned and at others so ornately decorated that it dwarfed even the oldest and grandest cathedrals in beauty? Steffy had to swallow her instinctive fear of such an alien place as she wandered through it on stealthy feet.

She felt dwarfed. Overwhelmed.

There came the sound of footsteps as the corridor intersected with another. Steffy ducked down behind a convenient outcropping in the wall and was just in time to conceal herself from the group that passed by her. Three tall men, beautiful, strong and purposeful, marched by, silent as the grave, their faces solemn and grim. She wondered who they were and what their purpose was. They seemed overly serious and an air of danger permeated the space about them.

Taking a deep breath, Steffy rushed on down the corridor. In the back of her mind she realized how hopeless her flight through this strange underground world would be. She didn't know the way out. Perhaps there wasn't one. Perhaps the cloaked man's magic was the only way to and from this world. It didn't bear thinking on that she could very well be trapped here until the strange people at the petrol station decided her fate.

Less than three hours before, if someone had told her of monsters and teleportation and men who could make flames appear from their hands as if by magic she would have quietly signaled to security to have the wacko escorted from the club. But now her world seemed vastly different than it had such a short time ago. Now she knew there were monsters in the darkness of the night and that magic did indeed exist. Not that any of it mattered. All that mattered to her now was escape. Let this new world of dark wonders rest forever in her memory—she wanted no part of it beyond that.

She wanted out of this place. Now.

Out of breath, due to nervousness or exertion she couldn't have said, she paused and took stock of her surroundings. The endless hallway was dimly lit. She had noticed the light before, but she had not noticed from where the light source originated. Now she did and was shocked by what she saw. Beautiful, ornate metal sconces jutted out from the rock walls and upon them floated balls of flame. There was no torch, no candle, no match. Only a perfect, hovering ball of flame over each sconce that served to illuminate the passageway with magical fire.

The only way not to give in to an overwhelming sense of panic was to ignore the phenomena of the 'torches.' Steffy peeled her gaze away from them and gritted her teeth against the urge to sob in helpless fear and confusion. Concentrating on the familiarity of the music that played in her mind she fled further down the corridor, now pointedly ignoring her surroundings as she went.

The sound of numerous marching feet echoed up ahead. There was no convenient hidey-hole for her to duck into this time. Steffy looked about in growing agitation for an escape route as the sound grew louder, closer. Luck, it seemed, was with her still. There was a large door not ten steps behind her. She sprinted to it, threw it open, and ducked inside. Her breath rasped out of her lungs now, but thankfully there was no way she could be heard beyond the door. The wood was thick and strong. She was safe.

A throat cleared delicately behind her.

Steffy whirled around, a gasp exploding from her lips.

Four pairs of yellow female eyes regarded her in silence.

"Uh." What could she possibly say to get herself out of this predicament? "I was looking for the, uh…the bathroom and I got lost." She tried not to wince. That had sounded like an obvious lie, even to her ears.

One of the women laughed before she politely disguised it with a dramatic cough.

"You're a human." The words were German, as Steffy's had been, perfectly accented but still oddly alien from the feminine mouth that spoke them.

"You're not," Steffy said defensively, mind racing for some plan of escape.

The woman smiled. "I am Desondra. This is Agate, Fauna, and Levine."

The four women seemed non-threatening. In fact, their presence was oddly soothing now that Steffy was given more time to study them. "I'm Steffy," she responded, careful to appear as polite as Desondra—of the long platinum blonde hair and beautiful cat-shaped eyes—had seemed.

"I've never seen a human so closely before." This from Agate, a woman with wide eyes, a wide mouth, and wide hips. She sounded nice enough, but Steffy wasn't ready to let her guard down, even for a second.

"Shh. You're not even supposed to have seen a human from far away, Agate," cautioned the blonde-haired Levine.

"Well we don't have to be secretive in front of her, do we?" questioned Agate in a stage whisper.

"When have we ever told anyone outside of the Council, dunce?" said Fauna, who was much smaller and obviously younger than the others.

"Excuse their rudeness, Steffy." Desondra's voice was gentle, apologetic. "You see..." She paused for a long moment, then seemed to come to some decision as she continued, "We are the Council's eyes and ears on the surface world, the Territories. We are Watchers. It is our duty to keep an eye on things from time to time, to record noteworthy events that take place up above and report back to our leaders. Not even our own people know this—even my husband is oblivious—only the Council, our ruling body of lawgivers knows about our activities. You can't tell anyone."

"Who would I tell? Besides, I barely follow what you're saying. Are you telling me that you're spies or something?

"Yes. We three, and several others besides."

"Why so much secrecy? Why not just grab a newspaper or something? Why not just watch the news, or better yet, get an appointment with a local congressman to get your information?"

"We aren't like you. We're not human—you've already seen that. If we were to reveal ourselves so openly it would send a shockwave through your world. Chaos would ensue. We cannot have that. It is the safety of mankind that concerns us, so we must avoid detection at all costs, you understand."

"This is the weirdest night of my life. Of course I don't understand you. I'm too freaked out to make heads or tails of anything," Steffy admitted. How could she? Her mind was in overdrive trying to process what it had already been forced to assimilate during the night.

"I have a feeling you will understand everything soon enough." Desondra smiled. "Come. Sit with us. We have some cider to cool your parched throat if you like."

How bizarre, yet homely this all seemed. But Steffy refused to be fooled. She daren't drink or eat anything here in this enchanted place. "No thank you. I…I can't stay. I'm looking for a way out of here," she admitted.

The women exchanged meaningful glances and Steffy resolved to leave the room immediately. She turned and jumped with a choked cry. Somehow Desondra had left her seat and now stood before her, blocking her exit.

"How did you do that?"

Desondra smiled, her yellow-orange eyes burning with such innate cunning that Steffy almost feared her in that moment.

"Don't be afraid. You won't come to any harm here. We are your friends."

Steffy tried to pass but Desondra stepped lithely in her path, blocking her once more.

"Let me pass."

"I very much like your clothes, Steffy," came Fauna's voice from behind her. "How long did it take you to make them?"

Steffy never took her eyes from the formidable Desondra. "I didn't make them. They were manufactured."

"What does that mean?" Agate whispered the question to Fauna but Steffy heard it all the same.

"She bought it in a shop, pre-made," Fauna answered.

"Let me pass," Steffy gritted out once more.

Desondra sighed. "It won't do you any good to leave this room. The only way back to your lands is with us—and we cannot help you without permission from our Council—or with a member of the Traveler Caste, and they are all out on patrols. They patrol every night now that we are in open war with the Daemons. Why do you want so badly to leave, anyway? Surely you have not been treated poorly?"

"I don't want to be a prisoner here."

"Is she a prisoner?" Agate of the endless questions.

"Who brought you here?" Desondra ignored her friend, concentrating fully on Steffy as they stood toe to toe before the door.

"I don't know. Cinder told this guy to take me somewhere safe and here I am. But I don't belong here. I don't want to wait around. I want to leave."

"Then The Traveler brought you. He will be back with the others—Cady's team—when the dawn comes. Can you not wait until then? Will you not keep us company? Tell us stories of your world?"

Steffy's mind raced for a way out of the strange situation in which she now found herself. Desondra seemed intent on keeping her here and though she seemed nice enough, she still made Steffy wary. Desondra, though pretty and soft-spoken, was clearly a force to be reckoned with. Steffy didn't know what to do.

The door behind Desondra opened and a masculine voice broke the silence.

"She will have more time for stories later, Desondra. Thank you for keeping her safe and sound. Steffy will join me in the main room now."

Steffy tried not to groan with the man's words. It seemed she would have no say in anything that happened to her this night.

The man stepped into the light of the room and Steffy was afforded her first look at him. He was tall—did the men of this strange place ever not grow beyond six and a half feet? His hair was a shimmering platinum blond, not so pale as Cinder's but almost. It fell down to his buttocks, tamed with a leather tie at his nape. His face was strong, leonine, with an untamed beauty that instantly conveyed strength and an iron will to any who looked upon it. He stood tall and proud in his dark brown shirt and pants, which left nothing of his bulging muscles and masculinity to the imagination.

But it was his eyes, a bright clear yellow, which were the most unsettling. His face and form looked no more than forty years old but his eyes told a different story entirely. Looking into them Steffy was swamped with the feeling of limitless, ancient age. Her head swam with the heady essence of his immortal spirit as it flooded around her. A new kind of fear possessed her. How could this man feel so old to her and yet look so young? It was impossible.

A look of puzzlement and curiosity filled the man's eyes. It was as if he sensed her reaction to him and wondered at it.

"Come with me, Steffy."

What choice did she have? The man gestured for her to precede him out into the corridor and she complied. He followed her, silent and studious of her every move. Steffy felt his gaze burning down upon her before he took her arm in a courtly gesture and led her down the corridor. Instinctively she sensed that there was no hope for escape from this man. She was trapped.

Who would save her now?

* * * * *

Now that Steffy wasn't rushing through the corridors, trying her best to remain in shadow and secret, she could take more notice of the details of her surroundings. This place—whatever, wherever it was—was immense. As large as a city. Larger. The corridors were at least a hundred feet wide. The ceilings stood taller, even, than that. There were massive doors dotting either side of the passageway, and every several hundred feet or so there was an enormous intersection where the corridor would branch off into another one or into a large antechamber with blazing fireplaces and comfortable furnishings.

Such was the room to which the blond-haired man led her to now.

"Please. Sit. You have had a trying night, lady." His voice and words were so courtly…and Steffy was struck again by how incredibly old this man felt to her.

Steffy gladly sank into the deeply piled leather chair to which he gestured. At least she hoped it was leather…and not something more sinister like human skin. She almost laughed at how dark her imaginings had become over the course of the past hour. Though these people were strange and not a little intimidating, surely they weren't evil.

She hoped.

The man studied her intently for a long moment. His yellow eyes were surprisingly courteous in their perusal, if a little too thorough in their regard.

"You're very young under all that face paint," were his first words to break the silence between them.

Steffy bristled, though why, she couldn't have said. She was young and looked even younger. But to hear him say it…one would think he was disapproving of that. "I'm twenty-four."

"Your hair is dyed like that on purpose?"

His words were spoken so tentatively that Steffy was hard put to take offense. She fingered a thick, wavy lock of bright pink hair, which curled around her chin. It had been so long since she'd let her hair revert back to its natural brown that she almost couldn't remember exactly what shade it had been. Now her hair was black with pink chunks throughout. She'd been planning on coloring it the next day to something more adventurous. Toxic green perhaps. It was a good thing he hadn't met her after that particular dye job.

"Of course. Don't you like it?" she teased with a grin.

The man smiled, startling her. He was beautiful when he smiled. "If you like it then it is as it should be."

"Nice comeback. You're pretty smooth."

"In my position one would have to be. So. Your name is Steffy?"

"Yes. How did you find that out? Did you listen at the keyhole of Desondra's room?"

"I have my ways—though I'm not above stooping so low as to drop at the eaves. Actually, Desondra told me." He tapped his head. "Telepathically." He winked devilishly at her wide-eyed expression. The rogue. "I am The Elder, Tryton."

"The Elder? That sounds like a title. Are you someone special then? Someone of rank? A leader?"

"If my people would have a leader, then I would be he. But I am called The Elder because I am mature, and because I am a member of the Council, a ruling body that keeps order here."

"And where is here?" She didn't expect him to answer.

"Home. This is where the Shikar live when they are not at the Gates or in the Territories, fighting the Daemon threat." His features shadowed then, as if with pain.

Steffy chose her words carefully. "I don't understand what you're talking about. What am I doing here? How did I come to be here? What were those...things...that I saw tonight?"

Tryton sighed. "You have been unlucky in your adventures tonight. You have seen much. The Traveler—the one who brought you here tonight—could perhaps take the memory of it from you. I'm not sure. Even I do not know all that he is capable of at this point." He laughed softly, self deprecatingly, when he saw her look of puzzlement. "I wish that you had come to us otherwise, but...so be it. I will explain as best I can."

Steffy waited.

"You are a human. Homo sapiens, in the Latin vernacular. You live on the surface of this planet, with only the pursuit of the advancement of your species through technology as a common goal among you. Your lives are short—on the average seventy years or so. Am I accurate thus far?"

Steffy could only nod. She felt more than a little alarmed with the direction this bizarre conversation seemed to be taking them.

"Good. Cady has been teaching me what I have not yet learned—through negligence, I admit—about your kind."

"*My* kind? So it is true. You're an alien or something. You're not..."

"Human? But of course you realize? I am definitely not a human being. No one here is." His eyes glowed in the dim light cast from the floating sconces and the fire that cheerily burned in the fireplace. Steffy trembled as he continued. "I am not like you. But I am not an alien or a monster—please be at ease on that account. I am, in truth, a native of this planet, though of an entirely different species from you. We are known as the Shikar."

"I don't believe you. I can't. It's not possible that a species so like us has lived undetected in our world. It's impossible," she said flatly.

Tryton sighed wearily and sat in a chair opposite her. "I'm sorry, but your disbelief doesn't make it any less true, what I say. Our kind has existed here, in secret, since the early days of mankind. The Shikars are an older race than humans. Far older. Once, we lived above ground, but those days are past." His eyes dimmed, as if in contemplation over some long forgotten memory that still haunted him. "We retreated to this place long ago." He fell silent.

"How old are you?" she was moved to ask.

Tryton seemed to start from his inner musings. He sent her a rakish grin. "How old do I look to your human eyes?"

Steffy chose her words carefully. "You look to be in your late thirties. At a stretch, perhaps early forties." She fell silent for a moment, wondering if she should continue. The hell with it; she was never one to bite her tongue, even if it was in her own best interest to do so. "But you're not that young," she added at last.

"How do you mean?" He seemed very interested in her answer and she grew antsy under the probing look he gave her.

"I can see it in your eyes. You are as old as this place." She gestured to their surroundings. "Older." She shuddered.

"My people would tell you that I am roughly two thousand years old."

Steffy flinched at the idea of such an age but realized even that number didn't…*feel*…as old as he felt to her.

"Your people would be wrong. You're older than that. By far, I think." She was certain of it.

"And what would you know of it?" He seemed dangerous then, his countenance taking on a fierce look of…*self-preservation*?

"I can feel the age in you. I don't know how or why. But when I feel this way I'm inclined to follow my instincts. They've rarely steered me wrong. And my feelings—my instincts—tell me that you are very…very old."

"Perhaps your eyes are not so human, after all," he whispered roughly, and looked at her even more piercingly than before.

The silence stretched between, longer than before. Weightier.

"Humans are a strange breed and a puzzling one. You have your weaknesses—sometimes too many—but you also have your strengths. Strengths that are not unlike ours."

"You're losing me again."

He raked his hand through his hair. "I'm sorry. You've managed to surprise me Steffy, that's all. I am not often surprised." He sent her an odd look, one she couldn't easily interpret. "I'm too old to be surprised much anymore." He chuckled. "All right then. I will begin at the beginning."

As Tryton's voice murmured on over the course of the next hour Steffy's eyes grew wider. Her mind and heart quailed at the possibilities of much of what was revealed to her. She sensed that what Tryton told her was the truth, though she would have had it otherwise. The path of her life was altered forever. She was no longer bored or curious or excited. She was something that she had never really, truly been in the course of her life.

She was terrified.

* * * * *

Steffy lightly dozed on the chair before the roaring fire. Tryton had left her to dwell on all that he had revealed during their lengthy conversation and she was grateful for the privacy. Her mind was in a state of sensory overload. She was in shock. It was a very near thing to keep her mind and body from shutting down completely. Her surroundings had long since taken on a surreal quality that left her nearly numb—and yet still not nearly enough so. She was feeling too much. The music in her head was a desperate wail—the expressed sound of the loss of her ignorance of the world in which she lived.

There were monsters in the night. And they had a taste for the flesh of gifted humans—like herself. Tryton had hit her with the news she had suspected without acknowledging all of her life—news that she was still loath to accept. She was touched. Psychic. More specifically, she was precognitive—at least a little—thus explaining her gift for easily orchestrating pre-recorded musical beats and her luck at never getting caught during her life as a car thief. Little things, but telling things nonetheless, when coupled with Tryton's revelations.

It also explained how she'd known when her dearest friend was going to die.

Steffy tossed on the chair and sought the blessed twilight of her doze again, but the memories came as they willed, flitting through her mind ruthlessly. Only now the memories were more frightening than ever after Tryton had told her, albeit unknowingly, that she was to blame for her friend's death.

Raine hadn't heeded her when Steffy had warned her not to drive through the freak snowstorm. There hadn't been a forecast for snow that day—and definitely not one for the blizzard that Steffy had sensed would blow through with a fury. But the storm had come. It had taken everyone by surprise…including Raine, who had been caught behind the wheel when it had come upon her. Her car had veered off the roadway, rolled down an embankment into a wooded stretch of land and injured her to the point of death.

But she hadn't died. Not right away.

According to the search teams, Raine had managed to pull herself, injured and bleeding, from the wreckage. She had wandered in the midst of the blizzard, leaving a blood trail that went on for nearly three miles. She'd been strong despite her wounds to have traveled so far in the white haze, to have lingered for so long. But the blizzard had been brutal and merciless. It had taken Raine in the end, into winter's cold and unforgiving heart, where she dwelled still, and would forevermore.

Steffy shuddered and tossed again.

If only Raine had listened to her. If only Steffy had fought harder to keep her friend off the road. If only she had known that what she had feared would truly come to pass through this negligence. It was her fault that Raine had gone, because she hadn't impressed upon her friend the importance of staying put. Steffy should have found a way—moved heaven and earth at the least—to stop events from unfolding as they had.

Steffy had called Raine at work, warned her not to leave, that the storm was coming and would take her with it before it blew itself out if she drove home through it. But Raine had laughed, carefree as always, teasing her friend about her portents of doom. She had promised to be careful for Steffy's sake...but Steffy had known that once Raine settled behind the wheel of her car there would be nothing to stop the fate that awaited her friend.

Steffy had rushed to the wreckage. She had gone out into the blizzard, knowing full well what she would face in the fury of that storm, with the hopes of intervening to save the life of her friend. But she had failed. Raine had already walked into her death before Steffy had arrived at the scene. She had failed her friend, at the cost of Raine's life.

She had seen the wreck in her mind as it had happened—though at the time she had stupidly hoped it was just her vivid imagination that had played it out for her to witness. Tryton had set her right on that score—her gift had given her that vision. It had been a true one.

The sight of the accident would haunt her until the end of her days.

Steffy had never before or since had such a vivid *vision*, as Tryton had called it. She never wanted to again. Never. Tryton had said she was gifted…Steffy believed that, if anything, she was cursed. And now she was made to wonder if every human was cursed. Humans lived life in ignorance, never knowing or suspecting that in the shadows of the night there dwelled monsters that would feed on them like cattle. And the saviors who would protect the humans from their fate…Steffy wasn't certain that they weren't to be just as feared as the monsters. They loathed humans for their sloth and their greed. And, perhaps, a little for their fragility.

She had heard this loathing—this disgust—in Tryton's voice, though he'd clearly not even been aware of its presence himself. He would have hidden it away like a shameful secret had he known, Steffy sensed. Tryton prided himself on being the impartial guide, the wise one, the father. But he had shown her, willingly or not, that Shikars looked down on the humans they were sworn to save.

It gave her no comfort, this.

Humans were caught between the horrors of the night and the ethereal, almost godlike beings who would rather live below the surface of the Earth than to associate with them. And it had been this way for eons. Steffy was at a loss and the only way to cope with these revelations now was to doze in and out of a light sleep so that she could think things through to a conclusion that suited her. One thing was certain out of all that she had learned tonight.

Ignorance is bliss.

Chapter Four

Steffy awoke slowly, drifting in and out of her hard-won sleep. She had never been one to awaken easily or quickly. Sleep was a heavy blanket that often served to cocoon her during darker times. Like now. And she was loath to give up that protection, such as it was. Reality was often a harsh place. Her heavy lids lifted, then shuttered. Lifted, shuttered…then flew open in surprise. She gasped.

Cinder was sitting in the chair opposite her, looking at her with steady, probing eyes.

"You're awake."

"You scared the hell out of me," she accused with a grumpy scowl.

"I like watching you sleep. When your mouth isn't spilling venom, your face relaxes and looks almost," he paused and seemed to search for the word, "exotic. Ethereal. Pretty."

His words caused warning bells to sound in her mind and she fidgeted nervously, sitting upright in the chair that had served as her bed for the past few hours. She couldn't meet his eyes or the heat that burned within their depths. After the night she'd spent, she wasn't quite ready for that.

"What time is it?"

"It is early morning. Dawn has burned its rays across the horizon of your city, bringing the battles of the night to an end. At least in that part of the world."

"Tryton said you can't go out in the sun, that most Shikars will get horrible sunburn if they do. Does that mean I'm stuck here until tonight?" The true question she wanted answered was left unspoken.

Would she be allowed to leave this place…ever?

"Tryton told you much of our kind." It wasn't phrased as a question. He sounded close to disapproving of the fact.

"He didn't tell me anything that would jeopardize your people, if that's what has you looking so irritable. And besides, no one would believe me if I repeated all that I've learned anyway."

"So reassuring of you to say so. When just a few hours ago you were full of bravado and bad attitude. Are you afraid of what I might do to you, now that you know so much? Is that why you are being so cautious and reassuring now?"

"Are you afraid that a lowly *human* could bring the truth of your kind into the light of our world?" she countered. "That it might make any kind of impact on your existence if one did?"

Cinder smiled, and it lent his face a boyish quality that was so attractive to Steffy that her heart thudded in a new rhythm, making her feel light-headed and not a little antsy. But his smile vanished as quickly as it had come. Cinder, she was learning, could look either fierce and dangerous, or completely guileless and friendly. It was an odd, unsettling experience to see the animated play from one extreme to the other on his handsome face. He was a man of unplumbed depths that could be deadly…no matter the mood he was in.

"You shouldn't have followed me, Stefany."

"If I had known what was going to happen, I wouldn't have," she admitted.

"So I guess the question now is...where do you go from here, eh?"

"Will I be allowed to leave this place? Unhurt?" The words felt like lead in her mouth.

"I don't know what Tryton plans for you now. You know too much about us, I think, to just let you walk away."

"Thanks for the reassurance."

"Would you have me lie?"

"No," she allowed.

"There is much at stake here, something far bigger than you or I. To let you go now is a risk. Everyone knows it is a risk. How can we trust you?"

"You mean, how can you trust a *human*?"

"Yes. In our experience it seems that humans are not the most faithful in keeping secrets and they can be dangerous in large numbers. You could incite a riot against us if you chose, of that I have no doubt after seeing the way the crowd in the club responded to you. You could expose us, endangering our kind—as well as yours—in the doing. You are a risk and not a small one at that."

"But I don't want to be a risk, don't you see that? I would keep the secret of the Shikars and this place forever. You have nothing to fear from me."

Cinder leaned forward in his chair, studying her. The air around his body seemed to shimmer, like waves of heat baking off hot asphalt in the sun, and Steffy was reminded of the power this man wielded. He could burn things, set them ablaze, simply by touching them. He could probably kill her with a touch.

She clenched her jaw against a moan of fear. She was no coward, she reminded herself. He may be strong and he may have an elemental power that could turn her to ash if he chose to wield it, but she was smart and she was fast. If it came to it, she felt confident that she could at least outrun or outmaneuver him long enough to seek safety.

But she prayed that it wouldn't come to such a thing between them.

"No matter your reassurances, you were in the wrong place at the wrong time, and Tryton will be the one to decide your fate. But for now, I can give you the reassurance that you will not be hurt."

"So you're promising me that if you have to kill me you'll make it painless?"

Cinder laughed suddenly and the firelight, which burned as brightly now as it ever had through the night, glinted on the mirth in his eyes.

"Do you think that we are so ruthless as to kill you to keep you silent? No. We are not without mercy. I don't know what your fate is to be, but I know it is not death. I wouldn't allow it." His eyes changed and burned into her once more.

"*You* wouldn't allow it?"

"I see the fire of life that blazes within you. I marvel at its brightness even as I wonder at such a flame captured in a frail human form. Your light will not diminish through death at our hands. I couldn't countenance such a waste."

Steffy felt some small measure of relief at those words. "Then what shall I do…for now?"

"Would you like a bath? The paint on your face must be uncomfortable after so many hours and trials."

She couldn't keep from rolling her eyes in exasperation. "Don't Shikar women use make-up? You all seem obsessed enough to comment on mine."

"It is an oddity, your face paint. Make-up," he amended, using the words as if they were alien on his tongue—and they probably were, she realized. "I've seen many human women," the velvety way he said this made Steffy well aware that he'd done more than *look*, "and some have used Make-up, but never with so heavy a hand. Or such a flair for the dramatic."

She let it go. "I would like a bath, yes."

"Follow me then."

Cinder rose to his full height. Steffy had forgotten just how small he made her feel, how fragile. She hated the feeling, but gritted her teeth and joined him as he walked from the room. His legs were long and well muscled beneath the tight leather pants he wore and they ate up the distance quickly. Steffy was hard pressed not to trot in order to keep up with him, she who had long legs herself.

It was with no small amount of surprise that Steffy found herself following Cinder to the room she had first been introduced to the previous evening. The room of iron and stone. She followed him through the door with a frown on her face. He led her through the rooms to what she assumed was the bathroom, where a large sunken tub awaited.

The fixtures were strangely fashioned but Cinder's motions revealed to her their purpose. Soon enough the tub was filling with steaming water and Cinder's eyes were burning into hers once more.

"I'll gather some towels for you." His voice had grown husky.

"Okay." Hers was barely above a whisper.

He was gone for no more than a brief moment. He returned with two fluffy towels and a large, masculine looking robe. He set them on the floor, next to the bathtub, and backed away with an enigmatic look on his face.

"There's soap for you on the rim, there. I'll just be in the bedroom beyond the door if you need anything else."

Beyond the door? That gave her no comfort. In fact it made her feel more than a little threatened. Cinder retreated, his eyes never leaving hers, until he stood outside that door. Steffy came forward and firmly closed the door on his face. She shuddered with something alarmingly close to…anticipation.

What a day this was turning out to be.

Heaving a sigh, she went to tend to her bathwater.

*****

Tryton had assigned her a private apartment, but Cinder wanted her in his domain. Here she would be under his power. Completely at his mercy, completely in his care. He didn't dare think on why that idea should thrill him so.

She was in his home. In *his* bathroom. Naked and in the water that filled *his* tub. She would be using his soap, would be covered in his scent because of it. The thought made his cock lengthen and grow heavy—heavier—in his pants. He'd been harder than a rock while watching her sleep, but he was miraculously harder now. He needed relief, and soon, or he'd end up ravishing her.

He palmed himself through his trousers. It felt good, that pressure, even if it was from his own hand. He pressed his ear against the metal door that separated him from the object of his obsession. For once he wished that he could tolerate wood in his domain—he would have been able to hear her better through wood than through this iron. But wood had a tendency to ignite in his presence if he wasn't careful. The only place he could fully relax was here in his home, because of the near absence of flammable substances. Thankfully, though, his sense of hearing was exceptional.

He heard the faint splash of water as Stefany cleaned herself.

He unfastened his pants, allowing his erection to spring free into his waiting hand. What he was about to do made him feel a tiny amount of chagrin, but the thrill—yes, even the danger—of being discovered by the woman he was fantasizing about was too much an aphrodisiac to fight against. He was shameless, even he knew it, and it felt so good to let his control slip like this. He settled back, ear to the door, and spread his legs comfortably.

Stroking his cock from base to tip, he shuddered. He needed to take the edge off of this lust and quickly, else he might just try to join her in the bath. He smiled at the thought, a feral flash of teeth had he but known it, and imagined her reaction to such a visitation. No doubt she would scream, or swoon. His member pulsed, his blood flowed like a molten river through his veins and his smile disappeared. He couldn't remember ever feeling so near to losing control of himself and his emotions. And *she* was to blame.

When he'd first seen her running across the battlefield the night before, his heart had stopped beating for a painful moment of sheer, unadulterated panic. He'd never fought so fiercely as he did then, in order to reach her side. He'd blazed his way through three Daemons to get to her…but even so, he would have been too late to save her if not for The Traveler. He hated knowing how close she'd come to death.

He'd wanted to shout at her for being so careless as to follow him. He'd wanted to throttle her for making him feel such a swell of fear. He'd wanted to fuck her silly for being so stupidly brave.

He wanted to fuck her still.

There came the sound of more water splashing in the bathtub. Cinder bit his lip against a groan and pumped his turgid length with a steadier rhythm. He stroked his hand down his chest, imagining that it was her hand doing the caressing, and arched his hips up into his hand. He trembled. His skin felt as if it were aflame with the force of his need. It very nearly was. His fire was so close to the surface, ready to unleash, ready to burn. But he kept it held in check, even as he began to gently rock his hips when his control over his arousal slipped a dangerous notch.

It felt so good to stroke himself while thoughts and images of Stefany's wet, slippery, nude body danced in his mind's eye. It would feel even better if it were her wet, nude body that was doing the stroking instead of his hands. His skin tingled and burned. He bit back a cry, stroking his cock, cupping his balls as they tightened against his body in preparation for release.

Beyond the door, Stefany sighed her pleasure over the bath. Cinder fancifully imagined that she was sighing her pleasure while straddling and riding his body. He choked back a moan. He squeezed his cock in an almost painful grip, felt the pulse of blood that filled his marble-hard flesh, and undulated his hips. One stroke. Two. Three.

He came with a flood into his pumping hand. The added lubrication of his seed sent him flying with a greater intensity as he continued to squeeze and stroke his sex. In his mind the wetness of his release became the wetness of hers, and he was unable to hold back the moan that issued forth in the face of such an erotic vision.

He fell back with a thud as the door opened behind him and he was left staring up, dazedly, into the face of a wetly dripping Stefany, garbed only in his robe. His cock pulsed once more in his hand at the sight, sending another hot flood of semen into his hand. One of Stefany's eyebrows—even more beautiful to him now that they were scrubbed clean of make-up—rose cockily.

"I think you're the one who needs a bath now."

Chapter Five

Stefany didn't know what to think as Cinder fell back onto the floor in front of her. Didn't know what to say. What he was doing was clear enough—listening to her bathe, masturbating to the noises she had made while doing so. It would have been a perverted thing to her…if it didn't turn her on so much. Knowing that he was so affected by her as to spy on her like that, made her feel powerful all of a sudden. More powerful and more feminine than she'd ever felt before.

Her tongue was tied as he stared up at her with his big, gorgeous Shikar eyes. So she fell back on flippancy, something that had served her well—and ill—over the years.

"I think you're the one who needs a bath now."

She saw the glistening white cream of his semen filling his hand; saw the impressive, nearly alarming size of the cock that had released it. It took every ounce of willpower at her disposal not to blush at the sight. His face, gentled after his release, stared up at her intently. There was a dangerous light growing in his eyes. One that sent pleasant chills up her spine. It was the look of lust. Of raw sex. Of want.

In an effort to distance herself, both physically and mentally from that light in his eyes, she stepped over him and passed him. Too late, she realized that in doing so she'd given him a clear view up the drape of the robe she wore, a view which no doubt was the reason for his swift, audible intake of breath. Damn it. It wasn't surprising that she'd been so careless. Her brain was a mud puddle just now. She wasn't thinking clearly at all, and was in fact operating on autopilot.

Steffy headed to the main room of the dwelling, turning her back on Cinder in an effort to steady her shaking nerves. It was a mistake, giving him her back. She didn't see him move, didn't feel him coming.

Steffy shrieked as she was lifted from behind, turned about, then slammed forcefully up against a wall. Not brutally, for it hadn't caused her any pain, but roughly still, all the same. Cinder pressed his length against hers, fitting his still exposed erection into the vee of her thighs with enough pressure to raise her up off the floor. His seed-covered hands gripped her upper arms tightly and his gasping breaths filled her ear as he rested his face against the top of her head.

Heat baked off of him in waves. Had he been any hotter he would have singed her robe off. Steffy froze in his embrace, not wanting to provoke his passions further, and waited to see what would happen next. The only sound between them was that of their harsh breathing.

"I want you," Cinder murmured in a deceptively gentle tone by her ear.

"I know," she croaked out, not knowing what else to say.

He leaned back from her, enough to meet her gaze with his. "Would you have me?"

"I don't know you," she managed.

"Your body would know me. It wants to know me."

Desire pooled low in her belly at the sound, the feel, of his words. At their velveteen timbre. She trembled against him. "My mind is not so weak as my body." Was that her voice, so husky and inviting even as it shook with nerves?

"Is this weakness? This storm that makes us tremble, makes us strain against each other in search of a deeper closeness?" His voice was almost a whisper, his mouth moving inexorably closer to hers with every word that was uttered. "My blood is pounding. My muscles are straining. But I don't think this is weakness. I think this is power. Power in its rawest, purest form."

He leaned in to kiss her, but at the last moment she moved her face away. He paused with his mouth only just brushing the down of her cheek. It burned her.

"Call it what you will. Not an hour ago you were talking to me as if I were a child, condescending to me because I am a human, not a Shikar. Not an hour ago we spoke of what might or might not happen to me because of this very difference between us. You say I am a threat to your precious cause, to your people. And yet you want me. Well I don't want you." Had a bigger lie than that ever crossed her lips?

"You would deny me. Deny us?" His voice was a growl. "Deny this?" His hips ground against her, the hard ridge of his sex digging into her brutally. Heat blasted from him to her. He was like a furnace as his ire rose in a haze between them.

She turned her face back to his, their lips brushing with all the gentleness of a butterfly's wings. "I have denied you. I do deny you." She held her gaze as steadily as she could manage, locked with his, even as she began to fear the discomfort of the rising heat that blanketed them.

His teeth blazed white, clenched in a grin that was not a grin but more a challenging leer. "I will take you anyway. And you will thank me for it later."

He took advantage of the shock that gripped her at his words. His lips fell on hers with the weight of an immovable mountain, and her bravado was crushed beneath it. Losing all pride she thrashed in his arms, shoving against him, turning her head away from his kiss though it was inescapable. His arms moved around her, crushing her to him ever more tightly than before. He lifted her clean off the floor against him and she was granted the opportunity to kick his shins in her struggles.

He merely insinuated himself completely between her scissoring legs, pressed her back against the wall, and effectively disabled her attack. But she was fierce and would not be so easily subdued. Yes, she wanted him, or at the very least her body did. Her sex swelled and wept with want of him. Yes, she found him attractive, intriguing and deliciously male. But she was not ready for this.

Was she?

Steffy brought her hands up, laid the tips her thumbs on his trachea…and pressed warningly against it.

Cinder stilled. He pulled back, his breath hot against her mouth, which was moist and tender from his kiss. "You *want* me," he growled.

She pressed harder, digging brutally into his flesh.

He released her. But he did not retreat. He stayed there, his body pressed flush to hers. They both panted heavily for breath, each unsteady and unsure of the other and what would come next.

"*Scheiße*. Don't ever do that again."

Cinder stared at her, still and assessing, for a long moment. His eyes were like twin orange flames burning in his face, and the air shimmered around them—visual proof of the heat that sweltered between them like the bellows of a furnace.

Whatever he saw in her face must have made him rethink his strategy. "You're right." He backed away, slowly, as one would from a wild animal whose next move could be a danger. "It was wrong of me to press you so. But you surprised me in a weak moment—you were right in calling it a weakness. You know I desire you. I know you could sense it from the first. But I do not desire this. I would have you in softness and in passion, not in force or animal lust. I am sorry."

Steffy tried to stop the shaking of her hands, raking them through her still wet hair in an effort to hide their unsteadiness from his all too knowing gaze. "You won't have me at all."

He smiled, a small enigmatic look that warned her of the folly of her words, which he could only see as a challenge. "I will have you. And you will love it. You will scream with the pleasure I give you and beg for more when I am through…many, *many* hours later."

"You have the ego of a god or devil. But you are neither. You are just a Shikar." She sneered the word with all the venom she knew a Shikar would have sneered the word *human*. "I will not fall at your feet in a swoon for your affections. I have a lot more pride than that."

His smile remained and the hairs on the back of her nape rose in response to it. "Pride goeth before destruction," he quoted blithely. "You will yield to me. And oh, what a yielding it will be. My breath would stop to think of it."

"Let it stop. In fact, why not hold your breath in anticipation? Go on, go ahead, *please do,*" she bit out in a rush.

He only chuckled, and the sound echoed behind him as he turned and withdrew towards the bathroom—no doubt to clean himself after his explosive release. "If you wish to maintain the last of your modesty, you will need to dress accordingly for bed."

Steffy sneered at his retreating back, but her bravado disappeared with his next words.

"For I mean to join you there as we sleep."

* * * * *

She wore her boots to bed.

"Move over, you louse. And keep that pillow between us or I swear I'm going to do you some serious injury."

Cinder chuckled and settled his length even closer, brushing her legs with his as he did so. Steffy kicked back, connecting the thick heel of her boot with his shin, and hoped he suffered at least a little pain for it. He merely chuckled louder and moved against her backside in such a way that the pillow separating them seemed practically non-existent. Steffy felt her cheeks heat with a blush but said nothing else, suspecting it would only serve to amuse him.

The coverlets that Cinder had found for her—he'd told her with a wicked smile that he'd never needed the added heat of bed linens before—began to stifle her, fully clothed as she was. It took every ounce of willpower that she possessed to keep from kicking free of the covers. It was his fault; not that she'd give him the satisfaction of ever saying so. The man gave off heat better than a fireplace. The pillow pressing against her back was burning from his body heat and causing her own clothing to stick to her perspiring skin.

Damn it. She kicked free of the covers. It was just too hot to stay beneath them. Steffy let out a loud sigh and settled back against the exquisitely comfortable mattress, trying but failing to find a center of calm. How could she find calm? There was a predator of a man lying next to her, blatant in his sexual interest in her person, just waiting for her to show some weakness that would give him a tactical advantage in seducing her. Calm was the last thing she felt just now.

"Quit fidgeting. You need your sleep." His voice was a gentle brush of velvet in the shell of her ear.

Steffy batted him away and scooted closer to her edge of the mattress. She sighed deeply again.

"If you don't quit sighing like that, I'll give you a reason to sigh so loudly. One far more pleasurable than mere restlessness."

"Shut up."

"Make me."

"You wish."

"You know…all that shiny black stuff you're wearing gives me the most wicked ideas. How do you feel about whips and restraints and silky, slippery ointments, love?"

Steffy growled and jerked away from the teasing hand that caressed her PVC-covered hip. "Would you just please leave me alone? I said no and I meant it!"

"You're just torturing me." He groaned dramatically. "Teasing me."

"Look, you're the one who refused to let me sleep in another room. If you're tortured or teased it's your own damn fault. Now *please* let me try and get some sleep."

"It must be hard, living a life with no sense of humor."

"Are you completely insane? Not half an hour ago you were as serious as the Pope at Christmas and now you're acting like *I'm* the one who needs to lighten up."

"Half an hour ago I was hard as marble with need of you. Now I'm only half so hard. It's easier to be lighthearted when I'm not so horny."

"Geez! You sound like some archaic feudal lord one minute and a twenty-first century gigolo the next. What is with you?"

"What can I say? I am a man of many facets. Just as you are a woman of many facets." His voice grew serious, the teasing quality of it deepening to a decidedly dangerous timbre. "Why did you follow me tonight?"

"I thought you were in a gang or something. Up to no good."

"Do you always follow ruffians, just to see what they are up to?"

"I was just curious, that's all."

"Curious about me."

"And your friend." Steffy sat up in bed, hugging her knees fiercely to her chest as she tried to see him in the darkness. "You struck me as...very odd people. I wanted to know what you were up to."

"How did we strike you as odd, exactly? Did we look any different from the rest of the people in your club? Was it the way we talked or dressed? Was it our eyes? Cady assured me your people would assume we wore contact lenses."

Steffy thought a moment, choosing her words carefully. "I don't think it was any one thing about you. I just sort of guessed there was something strange about you. I knew it was probably stupid to follow you but…I felt compelled to anyway."

He was silent for a long time, staring at her with his strange, glowing eyes. At last he seemed to find whatever it was he sought so intently in her face. He settled back against the mattress. "Get some sleep," were his husky words.

"What are you thinking?"

He laughed darkly. "You don't want to know. Just rest. We'll have plenty of time for talk tonight when we rise."

Steffy sat in silence for many long moments. "Cinder? Are you still awake?"

"Yes."

"This war between Shikar and Daemon…it's really bad. Isn't it?"

"Yes. We've been fighting them for centuries, but the battles were mere skirmishes and they only happened at the Gates, which stands between our worlds. But now…now the Daemons are everywhere. At the Gates, in the Territories, in the many dimensions the Travelers frequent. Where before it was an ongoing battle it is now an open war between us."

"Tryton says they keep getting stronger. What does that mean…for all of us?"

"We don't know yet. It's true that the Horde is increasing in strength and numbers but we haven't lost control of the situation yet. We are still winning the fight against them."

"What do they want?"

Cinder's answer was long in coming. "Death. Darkness. Chaos. It is the act of destruction alone that seems to drive them most. They suffer in what they are and so they wish for all things to suffer as they do."

Steffy laid back down, careful to keep the pillow between them, small barrier though it was. It was a long time before she slept, before the music in her mind quieted and fell silent. But at last she gave in to beckoning sleep, losing herself in dreams that blessedly had no memory or time or place.

Cinder lay awake for many long hours, listening to her breathing. It was nearly sundown when Tryton summoned him for a meeting and he'd barely slept at all. Steffy was still deeply dreaming when he left her. She barely felt the soft kiss he laid upon her brow as he rose.

* * * * *

"I know what you're doing. I don't like it one bit."

"What do you mean?" The words were silky soft, a challenge.

"I don't know you nearly as well as Obsidian or The Traveler do. But I know enough of your ways to guess where this might be going. You have something planned for Stefany. You can't let The Traveler wipe her memory—if indeed he can do that as you so casually claim—because you have some other use for her. For her psychic abilities, small though they are. Don't you?"

Tryton sighed. "Can't you trust me enough to do what is right by the woman?"

"I know you have at least some softness for humans. That you love Cady as you would a daughter is to your credit. But Stefany is not Cady. Your softness will not extend to her—how can it? She is not a warrior."

"I know that."

"What have you got planned for her?" Cinder demanded.

"What business is it of yours what I do? What I plan?" Harsh words intended to sting, to punish.

"You are The Elder and I respect you for that. I do. I would lay down my life for yours, this you know. But Stefany is…"

"She is special to you." Tryton sighed wearily. "Already it has begun."

"She is human—fragile. It is because of me that she is involved with us now. She would never have followed me last night if I hadn't spoken with her at the club. I aroused her intuition by contacting her. I am responsible for her safety. I will not have her placed in any danger."

"She is already in danger," Tryton exploded. His voice echoed off the stone walls surrounding them.

Cinder took a deep breath and sought for calm. The thought of Stefany in any peril did not set well with him for reasons he didn't want to explore too deeply. "From us? But that is easy to rectify. Why not just let her go? She will share with no one the things she has seen, I am certain of it."

"It is beyond us now, my young friend. There are forces at work here that even I do not understand. The Daemons are aware of her now, of her tie to us, however new it is. They will come for her with all the rage of their kind and they will end her."

"Keep her here with us then." Cinder bit out the words, fear coating his heart. Fear for her. For himself. For the world. The Daemons were getting far too strong, far too quickly. None of them knew why or how, but there it was, the awful truth of it.

"She is a human. And, as you said, she is no warrior. So unlike Cady she has no real place here, not yet. And I doubt seriously that she would willingly stay here and give up her life in the human world."

"You would just let her go then? Into danger, into death, with no memory of how she might protect herself? We are sworn to protect humans. Sworn to keep them safe. Stefany is no exception merely because she has seen too much."

"We are not personal body guards. I cannot devote protection to one particular human, when so many are at risk that have not the eye of the Horde fixed so intently upon them."

"I don't believe this!"

"What would you have me do, Cinder? I will ask Stefany if she wishes to stay—of course I will—but you have to know that I will not force her to stay. I will tell her the risks, tell her some of what she might face if she leaves here. But to what purpose? She is human. She will choose her own way and neither you nor I can overrule her decision."

"You know she will choose her life above."

"Yes. I have learned well enough from my time with Cady that humans are often inclined to be stubborn."

Cinder paced furiously before Tryton, who watched him with his ancient and knowing eyes. At last he seemed to come to a decision.

"If she goes I will go with her. I got her into this. I will keep her safe."

"I thought you might say that."

"It is non-negotiable. Do not try to sway me."

"You are part of Obsidian's team. Would you abandon them?"

"I will fight with them when they have need of me. The Traveler can retrieve me easily enough for that. Cady is a good Incinerator—one of the best. Obsidian's team will not need my skills all that often, surely."

"But if it is dark in Steffy's part of the world during those fights you would leave your human charge unprotected by joining your team."

"What do you want me to say, Elder? That I will just leave Stefany to her fate and be done with it? I am at fault here! It is because of me that she is in danger at all."

"She is gifted. She would be in some danger regardless of what you have done because of that. But you are right. You know the cost of involvement with humans. You know that recently, in rare instances, the Daemons have sensed out those whom we have touched, and since Steffy is psychic to boot—the perfect food for their endless appetites—there is not much that can be done to save her."

"I will save her. I will protect her as best I can. It is better than nothing—which is what you would give her. I thought you had plans for her, as you did for Cady, but to just send her back… It is negligent, Elder."

"My plans are none of your concern, young one," Tryton said warningly. "What of your days—what of the sunlight? You cannot Travel between here and the surface on your own and I cannot have The Traveler make special journeys just for you. Would you be willing to give up your life here to protect hers? It could be years before your protection was no longer needed by her. It could well be the full span of her life."

Cinder gritted his teeth. "If Stefany will not stay here with us until it is safe for her to go back home, then I will stay with her until I am no longer needed. I will hide from the sun as best I can. I will find a way."

"So be it. You have made your choice."

Cinder offered a stiff bow to his leader and quit the room. He did not look back, nor did his shoulders slump from the weight of his new burden. He failed to see the mischievous smile that broke across Tryton's handsome, ageless face.

A smile that, had he seen it, would have made Cinder seriously rethink the purpose of their meeting and Tryton's machinations regarding Steffy and himself.

Chapter Six

The heated press of his lips to hers woke her. Her first breath upon waking came from his mouth into hers. It tasted of wild and potent masculinity. It was just as hot as the rest of him—burning into her lungs with all the fierceness he so blatantly exuded, even when he was trying to appear harmless.

"Wake up, my sleeping beauty." He pulled back, but only just enough to speak the words, his lips tickling against hers as he did so.

"I'm awake," she whispered, hating for the delicious moment to end. Hating for reality to intrude.

He pulled back but kept his eyes on hers as she opened them. "It's time to go home."

She sat up in the bed. "You mean Tryton is letting me go?" It was hard but she managed to keep the hopeful tone out of her voice, managed to sound nonchalant despite the fact that her heart was pounding.

"Yes." Such a simple word, but it raised countless questions in her mind, the way he said it.

"Will I..." She swallowed around a lump in her throat. "Will I be allowed to keep my memories?"

"Yes."

Heaving a sigh of relief, she ran her fingers through her tousled hair. "Great. When do I get to leave?"

"Soon. After you say goodbye to Tryton and the others."

His words seemed so shadowed, as if he wasn't quite telling her the whole truth of the situation or was hiding something important, but she didn't care. She was being set free, and after a night and day of pondering her fate at the hands of these people, she couldn't be happier. To hell with his strange attitude towards her, to hell with the unrequited lust she felt for him, to hell with this magical place. She was going home and right now that was all that mattered to her.

"Well let's go then. I've had enough of this place. I've been having withdrawal from my apartment's creature comforts." She gave a laugh, hoping he might join her and break the tension of the moment, but he remained stoic.

"Come on, then. They're waiting for you."

She rose from the bed and followed him from the room. She'd come with nothing but the clothes on her back and she was leaving with the same, except for a few dark memories that she hoped would fade away with time. Who was she kidding? She would never forget one facet of this place or the man who was now leading her back to Tryton's anteroom sanctuary. Cinder, above all of the wonders she'd seen in the past twenty-four hours, would haunt her memories for all the years of her life.

And she'd given up the chance to be with him, for however brief an interlude it might have been.

She wanted to kick herself for her stubborn pride now. To be with a man like Cinder would probably be the most pleasurable experience a woman could have. But then again, she also suspected that being with a man like Cinder would have completely ruined her for any other man. And that was something she had to avoid at all costs. She didn't want to give herself fully to any man, least of all to a man like this Shikar warrior.

She had enough problems on her own without adding that kind of heartache to the list.

The tapping of their booted feet on the stone floors of the corridor leading to Tryton's sanctuary became an accompanying percussion of the music that played through her mind. The beating of her heart kept rhythm with the noise and her breath was the chorus line. It was difficult for her not to speed up her steps as a new feeling of apprehension took her and increased the tempo with its urgency. At long last—and not a moment too soon for her frazzled nerves—they arrived at their destination.

A small group of people awaited them there.

"I trust you slept well, Steffy?" Tryton's words were spoken cordially enough, but the teasing glance he sent between her and Cinder made her teeth grit against a harsh response.

"Well enough."

"You met Cady and The Traveler." He motioned to the lovely, dark-haired woman and the tall, cloaked man she'd met the night before. "This is Obsidian and Edge. They make up my greatest team of warriors. They have killed more Daemons than can be counted and will kill more than that before the war with them is through. You can trust them with your very life."

Steffy couldn't help but frown at his words. "Why do I need to know this? Aren't you letting me go?"

"Of course. You are not a prisoner here. But I must ask—is this your wish? You could stay with us here if you like. You will have a comfortable life, and you will be treated with honor as one of our own."

"Thank you, but no. I have a life that I want to get back to."

"But you have no close friends, no loved ones. You told me as much yourself last night when we spoke. And now you know firsthand of the dangers that walk the night—dangers which you must caution yourself to now that the Daemons are aware of you. Would you be giving up so much to stay with us?"

"I've lived with the threat of those monsters in the world all of my life and I've been just fine." She ignored his words regarding her solitary lifestyle. He might see her life as a lonely one but it was not, at least not to her. She much preferred having no one to worry over as she had worried over her lost Raine. "I can take care of myself. And I very much enjoy my life. I thank you for your offer of refuge but I assure you, I don't need it."

"So be it. Cinder will accompany you. He will be your guard until the threat is lessened to your life. His team will check on you both once a week, to be sure you are well and truly safe." He motioned for The Traveler, who moved forth, presumably to 'travel' them back to her home.

"Wait just a minute! I told you, I can take care of myself. I'll be fine. Cinder doesn't have to baby-sit me."

"But he does. The Daemons know you now and have seen you with us."

"You can't be serious. Didn't your precious warriors kill the lot of them? How could they know about me now?"

"They have a collective consciousness so if one has seen you with us then all of them have, you can be sure of that. I cannot, in good conscience, leave you at their mercy without protection of some kind."

"No. This is not cool at all! I'm not without resources. I'll buy a gun, put extra locks on my door, something. But I don't want a nanny, least of all that one." She stabbed her finger wildly in Cinder's direction, voice going hoarse as she struggled to keep from shouting.

"If you leave here it is with Cinder at your back. That is non-negotiable." His voice was hard as steel.

"*Scheiße*. I don't fucking believe this!" She'd ended up shouting after all.

"Take heart, Steffy. At least you have your human life to go back to. Think of last night, when you faced those Daemons and that life hung in the balance. Would you go back to that? With Cinder as your guard you can at least live in some safety."

"Fine," she gritted out. "But what am I supposed to do? Let him move right in with me?"

"That would be best, I think." Was that a twinkle of mirth in Tryton's eyes? His words were spoken so matter-of-factly that she assumed it had to be a trick of the light.

"*Scheiße*."

Cady came forward and took her hand. "We're only trying to do what is best to keep you safe, Steffy. Cinder didn't have to agree to guard you. Take it from me, a former human in the know, that this is probably the last thing a Shikar would choose—living with a human. Protecting a human full time. At least you have the consolation that Cin will be just a miserable as you." She winked cheekily at her.

"You are being given a great honor, Stefany. Cinder is a powerful warrior. He will take your safety very seriously."

"Shut up, Sid. Don't scare the girl," Cady snapped at her husband, then turned back to Steffy. "You'll be fine. And if there are any real problems, The Traveler will know and come at once." Cady sent a meaningful, commanding look in The Traveler's direction and Steffy was made to wonder—not for the first time—just who the leader of this Shikar team was. Cady or Obsidian? Could be either, or both, depending on the moment. "Nothing bad will happen to you so long as we can help it."

"Thank you." What else could she say?

Steffy felt rather than saw The Traveler approach. Cinder joined them. "Take my hand."

"If you should change your mind about staying here with us you have but to tell Cinder and he'll have you brought back. You have a home here now, Steffy."

"Thank you, Elder. I'll remember that."

She laid her hand on The Traveler's and Cinder did the same. The world around her faded away abruptly, then reassembled itself in the form of her living room.

"*Scheiße*," she muttered under her breath. She would never, not in a million years, get used to such a way of travel.

"*Scheiße*, indeed," Cinder said at her back. Steffy turned and was less than surprised to see that they were alone in the modern surrounds of her home.

The Traveler, of course, had already disappeared.

* * * * *

"How can you think with so much noise around you?" Cinder growled. He stomped to the stereo system, which was blaring at a considerable volume, and started frantically pressing buttons in search of some way to turn it down. There was a moment of silence, in which he grew hopeful of success, but he'd only succeeded in changing CD's and the noise was back at full volume within seconds.

"Holy Horde," he roared, clamping his hands to his head. He'd been too close to the speakers when the sound had resumed.

Steffy ignored him as best she could, going about her normal routine of mixing music for the club's sound system using software programs on her Macintosh computer. The stereo playing beyond her headphones—headphones that played the music she was in the midst of remixing—was just background noise for her. In actuality, she rarely turned it off, except to watch television or leave the house. But she didn't think Cinder would be happy to hear that truth spoken aloud so she let him fiddle with the buttons on the console in another vain attempt to turn it down. At least it was keeping him occupied for the time being.

How had she gotten into this mess?

She tried not to think about it. What was done was done. A fatalistic attitude was probably the only thing that would get her through the situation as it was. Concentrating on her music was what was important now. It was Monday, which meant she wasn't scheduled at the club until Thursday, so it was imperative that she find an outlet for her aggressions…or she'd end up attacking her bodyguard out of sheer frustration. She looped a few bars of music and winced at the offbeat caterwauling that sounded as the result of her efforts.

"What are you doing?" Cinder's voice boomed at her ear.

Steffy growled and jerked the headphones from her ears. "I'm working and I'd really appreciate it if you'd go find something else to do besides get on my nerves."

"What is that you're looking into, some kind of oracle?" He gestured to her monitor.

"No," she replied in disgust. "You Shikars know so much and yet so little about us humans. This, my friend, is a top of the line Apple Cinema Studio Display. It cost me a very pretty penny too, so keep your meat hooks off of it."

"You sound so much like Cady sometimes it's scary."

"That's probably because I spent some time in the States where she's from. I use a lot of slang, like she does. Most Germans don't sound like me," she explained.

"So humans are different depending on where they are from. I've always suspected as much. But as the years pass it seems that most humans become more and more alike."

"And I suppose that means you're old, like Tryton, to speak so casually of what basically amounts to human evolution."

"No, I'm not nearly so old as The Elder." He laughed, seemingly happy now that he'd gained her undivided attention. He plopped down on the couch situated a few feet from her and spread his length out onto it. His legs extended off the edge by a good foot or more.

"How old are you then?" She was almost too afraid to ask.

"Seventy-nine this winter."

"Good grief." She tried not to gawk. He looked great for his age, that was for sure. Just how long did Shikars live, anyway? She wondered at it.

"Am I too old for you, do you think?" He winked.

"Positively ancient." She grinned devilishly. "You couldn't keep up with me, old man."

His eyes burned over her, lingering on her lips, breasts and legs peeking out from beneath the table where she sat. "I think I could surprise you. Why don't we try and find out?"

"Why don't we not," she said with a wry twist of her lips. She was growing more and more at ease with these teasing moods of his. It was his more dangerous, seductive, and downright sexy moods that she was wary of now.

He released a long-suffering sigh. "Have it your way then." He folded his hands atop his head and closed his eyes.

"I will. So. How did Cady go from being a human to being a Shikar? Tryton never said how that happened, exactly."

"Her husband brought her over to us."

"How?"

"It is not for me to tell you."

"Is it something only Obsidian can do? Some kind of Shikar magic?"

"Tryton thinks we all have the ability to do it. But only Obsidian has ever tried, to my knowledge."

"You're avoiding telling me exactly how it works, aren't you?" she said in amazement. "After all I know about your kind, you would still keep things secret? Are you afraid I'd tell someone?"

"No. I just don't want to tell you." He flashed her a grin, but the look in his eyes was far too serious for the smile to reach there.

"Why not?"

"I could always show you. That would, perhaps, be easier."

"And become an overbearing, arrogant Shikar? No way. You can keep your dumb ol' secrets. I didn't want to know that badly anyway," she lied. Her fingers began tapping out a new rhythm on the table. She put her headphones back on and spent the next several minutes inputting it into the software on her computer.

She felt his hands on her shoulders long before she sensed him behind her. He moved so fast! She hadn't even seen him rise from the couch. He kneaded her muscles, reminding her that she'd been sitting in the same position for hours.

"You're so tense. Does it hurt?" He massaged more deeply into her knotted muscles.

"No." Her voice had gone husky. "Yes. I don't know." She laughed softly, her mind lulled with the pleasure of his gently squeezing hands.

"Let me ease you." His voice held the secrets of every decadent boudoir he'd ever visited.

Steffy sighed and trembled beneath his magical hands. She knew better than this…but it felt so good. So sinfully good. "Okay," she whispered.

"Take off your clothes and lie down on your bed." Had a man's voice ever been so innocently seductive?

Some bit of self-preservation returned. "I'm not going to take my clothes off, Cinder."

"You can cover your charms with a towel or sheet. I just need to be able to touch your bare skin."

The massaging of his fingers through the covering of her knit top felt so good. It would undoubtedly feel doubly so without that barrier between them, she felt certain. "Okay. But no funny stuff."

Cinder followed her, *stalked* her, to her room. He suavely gave her his back as she undressed and donned a satin robe. Heat shimmered around him in a nearly transparent halo and she wondered at his mood, which seemed more than a little charged and dangerous for the moment.

She lay down on the bed, rolling to her stomach. "I'm ready."

Like a panther he crawled up the foot of the bed, over her body, and straddled her hips. He helped her free her arms from the robe, uncovering her shoulders and neck. Ever so slowly, he moved his hands upon the fabric, pulling it down further to reveal the line of her back. The ends he tucked around her waist, his fingers expertly, knowingly caressing her as he did so.

It was impossible to keep from responding to so seductive a play and she squirmed a little beneath him. Whether to retreat from or advance into his touch, she couldn't have said.

"Lie still," came his soft whisper at her nape. "Trust me and you'll feel such pleasure as to swoon with it. I promise."

Foolish or not, she gave herself over into his more than capable hands.

The heat of his palms on her shoulders made her gasp.

"Too hot?" he asked, and magically the heat lessened.

"No, just surprising." She sighed.

The heat increased once more, ebbing and flowing until it became a pulse that beat at her knotted muscles with a delicious force.

"How's this?" Such a harmless yet sinful sounding whisper, that.

"Mmmm…" How had she succumbed so quickly? So easily? She didn't know, nor did she care. His massaging hands on her bare skin felt far too good for her to care for anything beyond the magic of the moment.

His hands swept over the expanse of her back, leaving a trail of soothing heat behind them. The length of his fingers and the breadth of his palms almost covered her back completely, making her feel small and delicate when she knew she was not. He was so much larger than she, dwarfing her, giving her a feeling of vulnerability that she'd never before experienced with any man. She was at his mercy and it was so easy to surrender herself this way that she gave in without a thought to the consequences.

The heat at her back waned as he pulled away, resettled himself at her feet and moved his hands to them. She tensed as he cupped one, the gesture being far too sexual for her to ignore, but he eased her with a surge of heat into the sole of her foot. Her protestations died a swift death before they could be voiced. Oh, this was such bliss! Her toes curled around his massaging fingers and her entire body sang with an echo of the pleasure that radiated outward from where he touched her.

Cinder moved to her other foot, leaving the first one to mellow in its tingling state of relaxation.

Mind numbing warmth ebbed and flowed from his skin to hers. She moaned softly, unable to catch the sound before it escaped. Cinder chuckled softly. His fingers kneaded her steadily, and the pressing and squeezing motions of his hands echoed in all of her erogenous zones despite her languor. With light, teasing strokes his fingertips flitted over her ankle and moved upward to her calves. She sighed and stretched.

The temperature of the room had increased by several degrees.

Steffy began to lightly perspire.

Cinder sent more heat flooding into her muscles and she gasped with pleasure. With her defenses down it was easy for him to spread her legs with light pressure on the insides of her calves. The satin of her robe felt shockingly cool as it settled between her legs, onto her sex. His body moved higher, spreading her wider to him. She moaned a soft protest—the last vestige of her resistance.

He brushed it away with a burning kiss on the dip of her spine.

The fiery touch of his hands moved up to massage her thighs. It felt so good to let herself go, to give herself over to this seduction of the senses. She stretched beneath him. He settled closer to her sex, which pulsed and throbbed and wept with the growing ferocity of her need. The heat of the room rose exponentially and she gasped, pressing her burning face into the cool softness of her pillow.

"Your skin is like pale cream." His whisper trailed over her shoulder, his softly pressed kiss was an echo there as it died away. "It tastes better by far."

A lone fingertip whispered over the seam of her ass, all the way down between her legs to the swollen button of her clit. A zing of electricity blazed a pathway through her body, from her head down to her toes. Cinder pushed the hem of her robe up around her hips, exposing her fully to his gaze. She tried to close her legs but he was still wedged tightly between them, resting on his bent knees towering over her.

That lone fingertip pressed into her clit, swollen and wet with need, and sent a bolt of molten heat into her. She cried out brokenly. His breath was a flame over her back as he plied his tongue along her spine. His free hand began a tantalizing massage of her bottom, squeezing and plumping the globes of her ass until they too burned like the rest of her. Her clit was aflame. He pressed and rubbed it until she feared she would scream, the pleasure was that great. Greater.

Where before she would have pushed him away, closed her legs to him, she now spread herself wider to him. Allowing for more of his touch. Eagerness was a shadow of the feeling she was experiencing. Madness was more apt a description. She was trembling, her flesh feeling swollen, wet and full to bursting. His finger caught and stilled on the ring that pierced her labia.

"What's this?" His voice was a husky breath upon her back.

"Mmmm..." She was beyond speech.

He moved with the speed of a cat, flipping her over so that she faced him. He studied the silver ring that pierced her. His eyes were alight with the flames that burned within him. Fingers scorched her, stroking her around the ring, tugging gently upon it. Steffy spread her legs impossibly wider, inviting his touch.

"I love this." His hand cupped her fully. "Bald and pierced and wet for me." His fingers dipped into her, stroking back and forth from her clit to her opening with long, sure movements. "Spread wide, pink and glistening in the light."

His words drove her wild. His touch made her crazy.

Without any rational thought to the likely folly of the path she journeyed, she undulated against him in search of a deeper touch. Her hips arched up into his hand, his finger slid smoothly into her pussy and he burned her with the fullness of that penetration. Moaning, gasping, sighing, she took his finger deep.

A dark chuckle rumbled out from his lips. He leaned in closer to her and pressed a hot kiss to her navel. It was easy work for him to move his way up her body, pressing kisses where he willed on the sweat-dampened expanse of her stomach and ribs. The air around them sizzled with the heat that rolled off him in a growing torrent. The long finger that filled her, stretched her, curved into a hook and pressed knowingly against her core.

She flew headfirst into the clenching fist of an orgasm.

Her body squeezed and pulsed around him, milking his finger as it would have milked his cock of seed. An orgasm unlike any she'd ever experienced stormed through her, wracking her body with pleasure until it was almost pain. His mouth settled on her taut nipple, drawing on it, sucking on it. The burn of his tongue was a rasp of molten lava on her aroused tissue. A strangled cry was all she dared to give him, though she wanted to scream with the ecstasy of the moment. Her pride would only let her bend so much to the man who worked her body like an instrument he'd been born to play.

It had been so easy for him. So easy for her. He hadn't even moved his hand beyond that crooking of his finger and she'd been lost.

His finger left her, making her feel empty and bereft. She moaned. His mouth moved over hers, his words tickled there against her lips. "I'll be right back." He was gone.

The temperature of the room fell several degrees. The heat followed him into the other room. Steffy sighed and stretched, her muscles feeling more relaxed, more replete, than ever they had before. Her body pulsed with aftershocks of her orgasm. Diamond-hard nipples stabbed upwards, one moist and shiny from his mouth, the other aching for the same attention. Her clit was swollen, her pussy drenched with the wet flood of her arousal.

Cinder came back into the room as swiftly as he'd left it. A thick lock of platinum hair fell over one fiery eye. He was every woman's wet dream come to life. He stood beside the bed and held out a square packet with one hand. He traced its corner down her chest to her belly and sex. It was a condom. A simple, human brand of latex protection.

"Will you have me or no?" he asked, solemn.

She knew then, without a doubt in her mind, that he would just leave her there if she said no. He would deny his own pleasure after giving her so much with just a simple word of denial from her lips.

"Yes." A thousand times yes. She needed him to fill her, to burn her. There was no question of that.

He stepped back and the clothes he wore burned away to ash at his feet. Steffy gasped but it was lost as he pounced onto the bed, onto her, and captured her mouth with his. His body, hot as flame, settled down upon her. Broad shoulders, tight, smooth muscles, a flat, rippled stomach and long legs weighted her down into the cool cotton of her sheets. His sex was broad and strong, nudging fiercely in evidence that his need was as great as hers.

Tearing his mouth away from hers he settled back and tore open the square packet with his teeth. It was short work for him to roll the condom onto his erection. That the condom was made for fitting over large cocks was not in question for he was indeed as big there as he was all over. Steffy's dazed mind realized with no small amount of alarm that he had to be at least eleven inches long and thicker than her wrist at the crown.

"*Scheiße,*" she cried. Self-preservation came too late and she tried to scramble away from him.

Cinder growled and gripped her hips with his hands. Their skin met and burned. He jerked her roughly down to him, slapping her sex against his with the force of his movement. The root of him was heavy, thick and hot there against her. She jerked away again.

"You'll take me, Stefany. You'll take me," he crooned in an effort to soothe her sudden fear of his body. There was no way she would be able to take that and Steffy knew it. She kicked out at him, rolled to her side and tried to gain her feet. It didn't matter to her now that she was acting like a foolish virgin. It didn't matter that she was naked and wet and needy for all he had to give. He was built like a horse and she was no fool to think it would be a smooth ride for them once he moved to mount her.

Cinder laughed. His hands caught her shoulders and jerked her back against him. He wrestled her gently back onto the bed, face first. He held her there on her stomach, pressing her into the mattress while his other hand moved down to stroke the wet heat of her desire. He spread her pussy lips wide and his fingertips stroked her with expert caresses meant to soothe and gentle her.

It worked. He knew a woman's body too well for it not to work. Gradually she eased down beneath him, trembling as her arousal reached new and desperate heights. Two fingertips eased into the ring of her channel. Then three. Then four. He was testing her, stretching her, making her ready for the real thing. She was so wet, so swollen with need. And still he touched her, played with her.

"So wet and hot. So incredibly tight," he said raggedly. "I want you so bad, Steffy, and I'm going to make sure you want me just as much before I come into you."

His words thrilled her, teased her. The tickle of his breath at her ear was a stream of warmth as he continued to coax her, to seduce her with the erotic timbre of his voice.

Endless moans had left her hoarse, breathless. It was all she could do to keep from sobbing pitifully, so intense was her passion for him. She could have experienced a hundred orgasms but Cinder had his own objective and kept her from the release she craved. He was driving her higher, past any pinnacle she'd ever reached, until she was in a state of mindless need. Time lost all meaning as he continued to stretch and stroke and massage her sex. They could have been there for minutes, hours, days and she wouldn't have known it. Or cared.

"Stretch for me. Flood for me. Do you feel that?" He thrust his fingers in an out of her in a fluid rhythm. "You're so wet I could drown in you."

The magic of his voice alone was driving her to peak. The expert play of his thrusting fingers inside her deep well was edging her along a great precipice, moving her towards the greatest orgasm of her life. Even as her channel pulsed and squeezed in an effort to keep his fingers deep within her, he gently but insistently removed them, causing her to shudder and clench against their loss.

His hands came down beneath her, pressing against her tummy so that she lifted her hips back against him. The broad strength of his hands squeezed her buttocks and guided her into position. She felt the fire of his cock as it pressed into the swollen wet flesh of her pussy. There was a moment of near pain, a stretching that burned and beat at her, and then it was gone as the great head of his cock slipped into her, filling her. Her legs were spread wide to accommodate him, the flesh of her channel stretched nearly beyond endurance so that it wrapped tightly around his thick, invading flesh.

Steffy came with a strangled cry. She felt the muscles of her vagina gripping, pulsing around the tip of him as he rested there, seemingly patient for her to finish so that he could continue. Her body came down from its euphoric high, trembling, and her orgasm subsided to dull tremors. He gave her an inch of himself, splitting her wide with the thickness of him as he sank into her. Steffy came once again.

He gave her another inch, stretching her wider still. He gave her another orgasm.

When at last he rested full length inside of her, the cradle of his hips pressing against the back of her bottom, she felt as if she was literally choking on his cock. She was so full. So filled with him. He was heavy inside of her, pulsing and hot. Steffy had long ago lost count of all the orgasms she'd had and was amazed at Cinder's stamina. He rested, unmoving, inside of her. She tried to move back against him, but his hands were anchored against her buttocks, holding her still before him.

"Are you ready?" he asked.

For what? What more could he possibly give her after all she'd already taken? She gasped hoarsely and tried to move once more. He held her motionless and she groaned, feeling something close to despair.

"Are you ready?"

"Yes!" She would have said anything if he would just let her *move*.

If she had caught sight of the satisfied smile that twisted Cinder's lips she would have fought harder to escape him.

"Here I come," he warned.

His body withdrew then slammed back into hers. Steffy cried out with the shock of it. He repeated the nearly violent movement, his flesh and hers meeting with a resounding slap as a result. His fingers dug into the plump globes of her buttocks, grasping them as if they were handles fashioned solely for him. His body thrust, over and over again, until the bed creaked and slammed against the wall with the force of his pummeling.

The music in Steffy's head matched the rhythm and tempo of their mating.

Cinder's breath was a bellows at her ear. His body curved around hers, surrounding her with his heat, rubbing against her with every movement they made. His skin was taut, rippling with muscled strength barely held in check for her safety. The heat of his hands left her buttocks, stroked over her back, tangled in her hair and pulled her face back to receive his kiss.

"I've wanted this from you since the first moment I saw you," he growled against the corner of her mouth.

"Me too," she admitted on a broken gasp.

Body pounding into hers ever more fiercely, he deepened their kiss, stroking his tongue deep within her mouth, tasting all of her secrets as if it were his right. A surge of heat swept from his sex into hers, burning her nearly to the point of agony. His body thrust ever more deeply and his balls slapped against the crest of her sex, pounding her clit until it tingled and throbbed and stung. His hand tightened in her hair, his mouth ravaged hers.

Steffy jerked her mouth away and gave a wild, animalistic cry. Her body trembled from head to toe. She would have collapsed if he hadn't held her up against him with strong, bracing hands at her waist. Another wild orgasm ripped its way through her. It almost hurt, it was so powerful, so intense and all consuming. She sobbed into her pillow, wondering if the sensations sweeping through her were agonizing or pleasurable—but the line was too thin between the two extremes for her to even guess.

Cinder groaned at her nape, licked a hot path from her neck to her jaw line and lowered himself over her. His face was beside hers, burning her cheek. He was giving off so much heat she wondered that they didn't burst into flames. The strength of his hands swept up her back again and moved to brace his weight on either side of her head. The pillow bunched under his grasping fingers. He groaned again and pounded ever more fiercely into her shaking body.

The force of his orgasm flooded into her. She felt the bombardment of his molten seed as he came into the glove of his condom. The bed shook as he drove into her. A bead of sweat dripped from his brow onto her shoulder and sizzled audibly. He thrust once. Twice. And fell upon her, breathing harshly into her ear.

His hands left her pillow and swept her sweat-drenched hair away from her face. He pressed a gentle, surprisingly chaste kiss to her temple and stroked her from nape to hip as he rested, full length upon her. The storm was spent, they were replete, and then reality intruded.

What had she done?

Chapter Seven

Steffy opened her eyes and blinked away the sleep with lazy motivation. The first sight to greet her eyes was the scorch marks—the perfect brown imprint of Cinder's hand—burned into her pillow. Where his fingertips had touched was singed completely away, leaving five perfectly oval holes in the pillowcase.

The second sight she beheld was the gorgeous expanse of Cinder's broad, golden back, fully exposed to her as he slept. Her mouth watered. Her fingers itched to reach out and trace the deep crevice of his spine beneath his heavy muscles. It took every ounce of willpower she possessed not to lean over and lick the glistening ridge of his shoulder.

Argh, she was hopelessly ensnared. She knew it, knew also that there wasn't much she could do about it besides sit back and enjoy the ride while she had the strength. Which, if Cinder had his way, would no doubt be sooner rather than later. It was impossible for her not to smile over the memory. The cradle of her thighs felt positively, deliciously bruised. Shikar men really knew how to show a woman a good time, or at least this one did.

She glanced behind her and saw the litter of used condoms on her nightstand. She'd lost count of how many times they'd been at each other during the course of the day. There was no question that Cinder was an insatiable partner. He'd still been in the pink, full of energy and stamina, when she'd passed out from sheer exhaustion, the feel of his cock slamming into her body accompanying her into a deep and unavoidable slumber.

It was not a little difficult to rise from the bed. Her legs were unsteady and weak beneath her weight. There were red marks all over her body, whisker burns, burns from Cinder's excessive body heat, burns from his kisses and love bites. Her nipples were red as berries from being suckled on so long and so deeply. The joints of her hips ached from being spread wide to accommodate Cinder's body for many long hours.

She felt like a woman well loved and she was. Never in her life had she been so thoroughly pleasured. But Cinder had been wrong. She hadn't given in and screamed with the pleasure he'd given her. She'd sobbed, wept with choking breaths, she'd yelled and moaned for him…but she hadn't bent beneath his will. She'd kept a piece of herself separate from it all, keeping her screams locked tight behind clenched teeth. No way would she give in to him so easily. She'd already surrendered too much, too soon.

It was a small victory, that, but a victory all the same. She grinned smugly, but it was short lived as she was forced to limp gingerly to the bathroom.

The water of her shower was hot, nearly scalding, but not nearly so hot as Cinder had been as he'd loved her. Her muscles were aching and tired and the heat of the water helped to ease them just a little. Her hair fell dripping into her face as she rinsed away the sweat and kisses that coated her body with sticky sweetness. She leaned against the wall of the shower and let the water bead down her head, neck and back.

Cinder's lips burned into the dip of her tailbone.

Steffy gasped, choked on the water that flooded her mouth, and whirled around. Cinder sat kneeling behind her, looking up at her with his Shikar eyes, an almost innocent expression sculpting the masculine planes of his face.

"You scared me," she murmured softly. The sound of the water splashing on their skin beat a tattoo into her brain.

His lashes, long and spiked from the water, blinked slowly. Seductively. "I can ease your aches away."

Her knees nearly buckled. "How? Another massage? I don't think I could take it." She laughed nervously. Breathlessly.

"There's another way. Countless ways."

Did she dare? "Show me." Foolish or not, she couldn't resist.

Slowly, gently, he placed his hands upon the swell of her hips. He drew her closer to him, until his breath tickled against her stomach. The heat of his fingers kneaded her before one hand moved to her thigh. He lifted her thigh, draping it over his shoulder as he settled lower between her legs. Burning eyes looked steadily into hers as he lowered his mouth to the blush of her pussy.

The wet heat of his lips burned her, soothing away any aches—real or remembered—with that erotic touch. She closed her eyes and let her head fall back beneath the shower spray.

Cinder's tongue swept between the seam of her pussy lips, licking a pathway from her opening to her clit. His teeth tugged gently on her labia ring. His face buried deep into her softness and she was forced to grasp his head in her shaking hands to keep her balance. The water continued to beat down upon them as he whipped her flesh with flicks of his tongue and lips. She moaned and undulated helplessly against him, letting him take her where he willed.

The rasp of his tongue was a torment that was almost too intense for her to bear. There were no secrets he could not uncover, no treasure he could not appraise. She was fully open to him. His fingers came into play with his tongue, gently parting her swollen folds so that he could kiss her more deeply, more completely.

Steffy glanced down, blinking water away from her eyes and gasped. Cinder's eyes met hers unflinchingly, as if he'd been waiting for her to look at him thusly. The picture he presented was one so explicit, so blatantly erotic that it took her breath away. The lower half of his face was buried in her flesh, his mouth working on her so that he appeared to be drinking her, eating her. His lips, his teeth and his tongue—they played upon her like a storm across the water until the flood of her response filled his mouth.

Involuntarily she began to ride his mouth. She could barely stand yet she swayed and undulated against him until she wanted to scream with the pleasure. But she had vowed not to give him a scream—simply because he'd boasted that she would. He'd told her once that he couldn't resist a challenge and she was no different. She would not scream.

Her hips bucked against his face.

The scream lodged in her throat, became a gurgling wail instead. Her body clenched, pulsed, throbbed. Her orgasm swept her away, wracking her body beyond the point of pain until she was consumed in bliss. It was frightening the ease with which he brought her. It was magical.

When Steffy came down from her high Cinder was already sliding his thick, heavy girth into her pussy. Her heart thundered; her head swam. The strength of his hands steadied her as he began to thrust his cock in and out of her. Unbelievably she came again, almost instantly, as he began to increase the tempo and power of his penetrations. Short, breathless moans escaped her lips every time he reached deep into the core of her. He caught each noise with his mouth, licking at her lips in the brief silences.

With surprise Steffy felt him jerk free of her, felt the hot splash of his semen on her stomach as he found release. She reached down and stroked him as he came. His powerful body shuddered and trembled with the force of it. Steffy rubbed the essence of him into her skin, reveling in the knowledge that she could affect him so strongly. Another powerful spurt of hot, creamy come and he was spent, resting his head heavily into the crook of her shoulder and neck.

Steffy dipped her finger into the hot spill of his release and brought it to her lips. Before she could taste it, however, Cinder captured her hands and brought them up around his neck. "Now we both need a bath," she said, reminding him of the first time she'd found him coated with sperm after her bath.

He chuckled and took her mouth in a deep, passionate kiss. His hands trembled as they fisted in her hair, bringing her face even closer to his. The water ran cool long before they managed to leave the shower.

* * * * *

Two weeks passed in relative peace and tranquility. Steffy and Cinder spent their days in bed, loving and resting and loving again. Their nights were spent in a state of constant alert. Cinder wouldn't let her leave the confines of her apartment during the hours of darkness, unless it was to work at the club. Even then he remained always at her side, in a constant state of readiness.

There were no attacks. No signs of danger. Steffy began to wonder at the need for Cinder's ever present guardianship. Not that she disliked having him around. He was a wonderful lover. He was becoming a wonderful friend. But she hated being penned in as she was, hated being looked after, however pleasurable the experience was proving to be…most of the time.

Steffy was growing tired of having black poster board taped to her windows to block out all vestiges of sunlight. But she'd learned the hard way that Shikar flesh blistered and burned in the light of the day. She'd left a small sliver of a crack between poster boards on her bedroom window that first day and a hairline ray of the sun had left a red welt on Cinder's naked thigh.

She'd been sure to cover every possible peephole after that. The sun hadn't entered her apartment in a fortnight. Not that she needed the sun, because she'd always been more nocturnal anyway. The fire that burned in Cinder's eyes had become her sun, moon and stars in recent days. That was really all she needed for the present.

But that didn't mean she was complacent in her position of house arrest.

She missed her freedom. Her independence. She'd never spent much time with anyone besides Raine, had always led a solitary, private existence. But now she was being forced to let that go. Everywhere she turned Cinder was there at her side, and while it was usually a warming experience—figuratively as well as literally—there were times when all she longed for was privacy or a stroll out in the sunlight to a local café or shop. Cinder would have none of that. He felt it was still too dangerous for her to venture forth without him, too risky for her to leave the relative safety of her home.

Steffy had a horrible case of cabin fever.

And Cinder seemed no better than she. When he wasn't thrusting deep within her body he was prowling around the apartment like a caged tiger, checking and rechecking all the locks on the doors and windows as if he expected them to try and sneak something by him. He was obviously unused to such small quarters as her home, was more used to open spaces in his home and in his work.

By the beginning of the third week they had begun to grow testy with one another. Steffy genuinely like Cinder—she just couldn't be around him twenty-four/seven without feeling some agitation. The man was just too stubborn for his own good. And she suspected, at times, that he deliberately baited her out of sheer boredom.

"I'm not going to listen to that *Dead Can Dance* CD one more time, Cinder. I'm sick and tired of it already. Can't you find something else you like in all my music?"

"I've listened to most of your other stuff and this is my favorite. I can't stand the caterwauling of your other CD's."

Steffy growled in frustration as she watched Cinder insert the CD. "Try The Smiths, or Fiona Apple. Anything but this again, *please*."

Cinder ignored her and the haunting ballads of the band flooded her apartment. She gritted her teeth against the urge to shout at him as he plopped down in his favored position on her couch. She jerked out of her chair and began to gather her things for the evening ahead.

"It's a little early for that, isn't it? You aren't due at the club until ten."

She flashed a smug grin his way. "For your information I'm not working at the club tonight. I've got a gig at a private party."

Cinder shot upright, instantly alert, and sent her a hard look. "Where is it?"

"About a two-hour drive away." She relished the perturbed look on his face with wicked glee.

"Why wasn't I told sooner?"

"I've been planning it for a month. It's a well-paying gig with the possibility for more freelance jobs in the offing. You don't think I'd cancel just because of this perceived Daemon threat of yours, do you?"

"Are you mad, woman? Don't you realize the folly of such an endeavor? Leaving your familiar territory for a new one is sure to give the Daemons a tactical advantage should they choose to strike."

"It's no big deal Cinder, chill out." American slang, always there to save her.

"It is a *very* big deal. Daemons are becoming known for their ability to sense weakness—any weakness—and use it to their benefit. You are putting yourself at risk and for what? Money? Excitement? These things mean *nothing* when weighed against the value of your life."

"You know what I think?" Her voice rose along with her ire. "I think this whole thing has been a set up from the get go. A ploy to get me in the sack with you. I haven't seen hide nor hair of these Daemons since that first night. I think there is no threat to my safety. I think you're just here to get your rocks off." She didn't really believe that, but she was so angry she felt the need to strike out at him somehow.

Cinder stalked over to her and stared down into her eyes. The temperature of the room rose several alarming degrees. "You do yourself no favors in accusing me of such duplicity, woman." His words were biting in their formality. "I wanted you, yes. I seduced you, yes. But you wanted me just as much as I wanted you and we both know it or I wouldn't have pursued. I would have kept my distance all this time but for your willingness. Don't think to insult me with such harsh words, for I won't have it."

"Okay, okay. I'm sorry." She hastened to placate him. "I let my temper get the better of me. But Cinder, you have to admit that these past weeks have gone on without any sign of danger. I think you're wasting your time here."

"Would you have me leave you then?" His eyes were twin flames burning into hers.

"No." There was no question of that. "I just don't like feeling so trapped in my own home."

"If you came back to my home you would have all the freedom you desire."

"My place is here. My life is here. I'd be even more a prisoner if I went back with you now."

Cinder sighed and backed away. "The Traveler will bring my team here tomorrow night for their weekly check in. I will ask Cady what she thinks. She senses the Daemons far better than any of us can anyway. Perhaps you are right. Perhaps Tryton overestimated your allure to the Horde's minions. Cady will know."

The thought of his leaving her caused an ache to spread from her heart to the rest of her body. But she wanted her freedom. She wanted her life to go back to the way it was. Didn't she?

"Get ready then." Her voice was hoarse, strained. "We'll be leaving in an hour."

"Fine."

Steffy concentrated on the rhythms in her mind as she gathered her things and ignored the weeping music that resounded in her heart.

Chapter Eight

"Stupid heater isn't working," Steffy growled, her numb fingers fiddling awkwardly with the heat controls on the dashboard of her old Austin mini. She'd driven nicer cars in her day, it was true, but this one she had bought and paid for through honest work.

"Are you cold?"

"Freezing," she admitted.

"All you had to do was ask," Cinder teased and suddenly the confines of the car warmed up considerably.

Steffy laughed. "I forgot. Thanks."

"Anything for my lady."

The long country road lay winding and solitary before them for miles in the darkness. Steffy tapped her fingertips on the steering wheel in a ceaseless, ever changing rhythm, breaking the silence between them. Cinder had begged her to leave the stereo off during the trip. He couldn't stand the ever-present noise she was so addicted to.

"Are you hungry?" she asked in a rush. The silence was grating her already and they hadn't been on the road for more than thirty minutes. "I've got some hot dogs in a baggie in the back seat if you like. The last time Cady stopped by she told me how much you like them."

Cinder shuddered. "No thank you. I like my dogs better alive."

Steffy laughed. "You're so weird."

"You're the one who's weird. I know you like dogs—living dogs. You pet your neighbor's poodle every chance you get. How can you, in good conscience, eat something you love so much?"

Her laughter stopped. "Are you serious?"

"Of course. Doesn't it shame you at times, your penchant for ingesting 'man's best friend'?"

She roared with laughter. "They're not real dogs, you nut. They're just called hot dogs. They're usually made of pork or beef byproducts. No dog. At least… I don't think so." She frowned, suddenly thinking of those nameless byproducts that made up hot dogs. She'd never been much of a fan of them herself.

Cinder seemed to ponder her words. "Why would a food bear so misleading a name?"

"It's just a gimmick name, Cinder. I don't think there was any real intention by the inventor of these things to trick you into thinking it was a real dog."

"Humans are so strange."

"Shikars are the strange ones." She paused, took a deep breath, and finally spoke of the thing that had been bothering her ever since she'd met up with the Shikars. "I mean think about it. You spend most of your lives guarding these Gates of yours against Horde invasion and for what? So the Daemons will get wise and find a way to sneak past you into the human world. So then you spend the rest of your lives tracking these things down to protect the world from their evil threat. Why? You don't like humans. You protect us, yet you don't care for us at all. Why is that?"

"It's just the way it has always been for my kind."

"Why? Haven't you ever wondered why?"

"Well yes, I guess. When one is young, one always questions these things. But as time passes the why becomes unimportant." He fell silent for a long moment and then blurted out in an almost defensive rush, "It is my sworn duty to protect humans against the threat of the Daemon Horde. As you said, it shouldn't matter why. It just is."

"Why do you resent humans so much?"

"I don't resent them. I don't," he stressed. "But your kind confuses me. You are so oblivious to the world around you as it is. You seek to control and change everything you come into contact with. And yet you're so innocent as you do it."

"I can assure you that most of us aren't innocent at all in the things we choose to do," she said wryly.

"But you are. There are so many wonders that you are unaware of, my kind being the least of them. But you would do anything to live in ignorance of those wonders. You have no pride in your race, only in yourselves as individuals. Your history seems to have no value outside of the schoolroom. Nothing matters to you but your immediate pleasures. You live so short a time and struggle so hard to ignore that fact. You should make every moment of your life count for all it is worth. But most of you throw it away on frivolous, meaningless pursuits."

"Like me, you mean. I entertain people for a living. People who are 'throwing away their lives in the pursuit of pleasure' as you said."

"That's not what I meant."

"It *is* what you meant."

"Your music is brilliant. You are brilliant. But where you could be orchestrating your own music, you are remixing the music of others. And where you could be sharing your gift with the masses, you choose instead to share it with a few drunken wildlings at a small club in the middle of nowhere."

"Hamburg is not in the middle of nowhere."

"You know what I mean. You have potential and yet you do nothing to obtain the fullness of it."

Steffy thought for a moment, his words bringing her no small amount of pain. "You're right." Her voice was weak with the realization. "I'm not really trying. But I tried once, went to college, studied hard, tried to train for a professional career in a recording studio. It didn't work out. Nothing like that ever works out for people like me."

"What do you mean, for people like you?"

"A nobody. A loser. I came from nothing. From trash. My mother lit out when I was three, leaving her family for one of her endless string of boyfriends. I haven't seen her since. My dad was an asshole who hit me every chance he got, after she left, in order to feel like he actually controlled at least one thing in his life. I left home as soon as I could get out of school and lit out on the streets because I had nowhere else to go. I thought I could make it fine on my own, thought I was so smart." She sniffed derisively.

"It wasn't a week before I was into some pretty shady stuff. A couple of weeks and I was part of a street gang, a ring of car thieves. I was pretty good at it. I had an instinct for when cops or security might be close. I liked to steal cars right off the lots of the dealerships—I hated stealing directly from people, as lame as it sounds. I stole prime pieces only because it was all a game to me at the time. I still hold the record for the most scores in one night. Not that I'm proud of that," she hastened to add.

"How did you get away from such a life?" he asked gently.

"One day I woke up and realized there was no future for me beyond jail or rape or a knife in my stupid back. So I took some money I had saved up—money I'd earned from stealing and stripping cars—enrolled in a foreign school and left on the earliest available flight to America. I was lucky, really lucky, that I had my academic history to fall back on. People tend to ignore any minor red flags when you possess the right I.Q."

"Then I was wrong. You haven't wasted yourself. You've come a long way in your years. I am sorry."

She snorted inelegantly. "Be still my heart. An apology? From you? There must be icebergs at the Gates right now." They laughed together. "But you're right. I'm not really going anywhere. I am having fun though, so that's something, I guess." She smiled at him.

The car sputtered and jerked beneath them. Steffy downshifted in an effort to rev the engine, but to no avail. The car shuddered, coughed and died.

"What the hell?" She tried to turn the engine over, pumping the gas as she did so. The engine caught, held, then died again. Steffy tapped on the gauges behind the wheel and groaned as the fuel gauge's needle abruptly fell from half a tank to empty. "Damn it. I thought they fixed that at the garage when I took this in for service."

"What is it?" Cinder's voice was alert, ready for action.

"Fucking petrol meter doesn't work. I told the mechanic to fix it. The asshole charged me for labor on it so it should work."

"What are you talking about?" he asked slowly, as if talking to a fussy child.

Steffy glared at him. "We're out of gas. And we're probably miles away from the next petrol station."

"Can't you use your cell phone to call for help?"

Steffy was way ahead of him; had, in fact, pulled her cell phone out of her purse before the words left his mouth. She pressed the button to illuminate the face and groaned at the message that greeted her.

No service.

"We're too far out of range. My coverage doesn't extend all the way out here, I guess, or the phone just can't get a signal through all these hills."

"Do you mean we're stuck here?" he growled dangerously.

"We'll have to flag somebody down."

"There's no one on this forsaken road for miles, in case you haven't noticed. I know I can see farther than you but you can at least see that much."

"Don't raise your voice to me."

"I'm not raising my voice," he nearly shouted, slamming a fist on the dash for emphasis.

"There will be more traffic on this road come morning."

"I can't be out here come morning," he gritted out.

"*Scheiße*. Sorry. I'm flustered, I forgot. Well." She took a deep breath and tried to think. "It's early yet, barely eight o'clock. We'll give it a couple of hours and if no one has driven by we'll walk to the nearest house. There are farms dotted all around this area. There's bound to be a home somewhere near enough for us to reach it easily enough on foot."

"You foolish woman. I told you this trip was folly."

"I'm sorry, okay? There's no reason to get uptight about it. We'll cope."

She shivered despite the rising heat that baked off of Cinder's body. For all the harshness of Cinder's admonitions they didn't compare to the harshness of her own. How could she have been so foolish? She'd placed Cinder's life in danger by coming out here. What if they couldn't find shelter before morning?

They would, she vowed. They had to. Cinder meant too much to her for her to let such a horrible thing happen without putting up a hell of a fight.

She opened her door and exited the vehicle. In a vain effort to capture a signal she walked several yards ahead of the car, raising her cell phone high in the air. When she had no luck there, she retraced her steps, then walked several more yards in the opposite direction.

There was still no signal.

"*Scheiße*! Damn it. *Scheiße*." She stomped her foot and winced. Her toes had long since gone numb and needle-sharp pain was her only reward for the childish gesture. "Fuck," she growled.

She walked gingerly back to the vehicle and collapsed inside, shivering from the cold. "I can't get a signal out here," she griped.

Reaching over his lap and into her glove box she retrieved an old forgotten package of black clove cigarettes and placed one between her lips. Her cold fingers almost dropped the lighter she fished out of her purse, and after several fruitless attempts to light her clove she growled in frustration.

"I can't get my fingers to work," she complained to Cinder, who was watching the whole process with a small smile. "The stupid thing won't light," she mumbled, causing the cigarette—still perched between her lips—to bounce precariously.

Cinder reached out and placed the tip of his index finger to the end of her clove. A tiny spark appeared and a thin stream of smoke began to drift upwards. She drew deeply upon it, not a little unnerved by the display, and he removed his finger.

"Thanks," she said hoarsely.

"Anytime," was his suave response.

The clove served to warm her a little, as she'd hoped it would. The gentle perfume of the herb filled the automobile with a welcoming sweetness. They settled back to wait, their eyes watching the road intently before them in search of approaching headlights.

Chapter Nine

"You're cold. Come here and I'll warm you." His voice was pure, wicked seduction.

"How can you think about sex at a time like this?" She laughed, heart already racing with anticipation.

"What better time to think of so pleasurable a thing as now when we find ourselves in this uncomfortable situation?"

Steffy snorted but it was a feeble effort. Her nose was too cold for it.

"Think of it as a practical survival endeavor. If I give off too much more heat I'll scorch your seat and it still won't sufficiently warm this car. It's not airtight. There are too many drafts." He reached out and touched his burning finger to her cheek, stroking her softly. Shamelessly tantalizing her with the lure of his warmth.

"There's no room for it. The backseat and boot are full of my equipment."

"There's room enough." He pushed his seat back as far as it would go and patted his lap. "Climb on. I'll help you."

Steffy giggled—*actually giggled*—and wondered if perhaps she was losing her mind. "You'll help me?"

"Come on. It'll be fun. And it will relax us both so that we can think of a good plan."

"You are so cute when you're horny." She laughed and began to disrobe, then thought better of it. "I'll get too cold."

"No you won't. Take them off, I'll keep you warm."

"Promise?" she teased, already removing her garments.

"I promise." His teeth were a white blaze in the darkness as he leered at her devilishly.

"I can't believe I'm doing this," she muttered as she peeled away her red stockings and black silk panties. Her skirt—a red and black plaid mini with silver loops adorning it—she left on.

"Oh, I like that," he breathed appreciatively, rubbing her bared thighs as she awkwardly crawled over him.

"I thought you might," she said impishly.

Cinder's hands went to the fastening of his pants, and it was short work before his erection sprang free and strong away from its confines. He produced a condom from the confines of one pocket—Steffy was amazed that he never seemed to be without protection—and rolled it over his straining thickness. He helped to guide her legs to either side of him, and held the base of his cock steady as she wriggled down onto him.

The sleek wet softness of her body eased his way despite the tight fit and they sighed with the pleasure of it.

"Warm me, Cinder." She breathed her siren's call into his mouth.

His arms came around her, moving beneath her blouse, surrounding her with heat. He wore short sleeves—he always did, because he had no real need of heavier clothing. His golden muscles bulged as he pulled her closer to him, stroking from her back to her thighs in long, sweeping motions.

"You have the longest, sexiest legs I've ever seen. Have I told you that?"

"Only about a hundred times," she laughed, "but still not nearly often enough."

"I just want to wrap them around my neck and drown in you," he said thickly.

Her nipples peaked at his words. "I love it when you say such things," she gasped, fitting herself more fully onto his marble-hard cock.

"I have to see your breasts," he muttered darkly, gaze boring into her chest as if he could burn away the covering.

Steffy realized that he very probably could.

Her fingers moved swiftly to unbutton her chaste cotton shirt and Cinder's hands pulled down the lace of her bra to bare her to his gaze. He sighed and palmed her.

"They're like hard apples in my hand," he growled and pressed a hot kiss to her arching neck as she leaned into his touch.

"They're too small," she moaned. His hands dwarfed her.

"Perfect." His fingers tugged on her stabbing nipples.

The smooth, sleek feel of the condom he wore slipped deeper inside of her. Steffy would have sworn that he reached as far as the back of her throat, so deeply did he penetrate her body. She felt spitted, impaled. It was a delicious feeling and one she'd grown hopelessly addicted to over the course of the past two weeks.

His hands moved beneath her breasts to her ribs where he gripped her, lifted and lowered her, helping her to begin the hard, bouncing ride he knew would drive her wild. Her breasts bobbed before him until he gave in to the temptation to draw one into his mouth. Strong, white teeth rolled her nipple. The burn of his tongue rasped her, the moist caress of his breath played over her skin until it trembled.

With shaking, desperate hands, Steffy clenched his head ever more tightly against her. His hair was like silk in her fingers, a spill of platinum fire that glinted in the darkness. The gold-dusted tips of his lashes brushed her skin as he buried his face into the swell of her breast, tickling her, caressing her with his every movement. Steffy dug her pelvis into him on a down stroke, burying him deeper inside of her. They both gasped their response, shuddering in unison.

The dripping wet heat of her pussy gripped him, pulsed and squeezed around him like a tight fist. The crown of his cock swelled and filled her so tightly that their bodies made wet, slurping sounds as they thrust back and forth. The blood that engorged him was so hot as to nearly scald her insides, scraping against her G-spot with that heat until she was mewling her ecstasy aloud in response to every deep stroke he made within her.

Cinder bucked up into her even as he moved her upon him until the car shuddered and rocked with the force of their movements. Ever the lover of rough play, he pounded into her with the force of a battering ram. Steffy groaned and held on for dear life. He was like a storm upon her, wild and untamed and fierce. Steffy moaned, cried, and whimpered…but she didn't scream.

"Scream for me," he demanded, moving his mouth to hers, parting her lips as if he could draw the surrender from her.

"No." She trembled. She burned. But she wouldn't scream for him.

"You *will* scream for me."

Steffy gritted her teeth against the primitive, womanly urge to obey her man.

His tongue licked her lips, a brush of fire. She moaned. The fire flowed into her mouth, licking her teeth and tongue with long, demanding strokes. His lips slanted over hers. His hips pounded ever more fiercely into her, his hands pulled her down onto him with bruising force. The burn of his fingers scorched a path down to her hips, beneath her skirt, and dug into the soft handle of her buttocks.

He spread her wide, rubbed his finger over the pucker of her anus, and she jerked against him. The hot, wet pulse of her release took her in a rush until she was mindless in the path of that all-consuming pleasure.

But she didn't scream.

She swallowed the urge, tamped it down before it could escape and give him the satisfaction his ego demanded so mercilessly. A groan bubbled up from the depths of her body, the sound one of deepest satisfaction. And triumph. Triumph that she'd still—after all this time, after all this battling—succeeded in keeping some small piece of herself from him.

Cinder growled and bit her lip in punishment. The love bite only added to her pleasure; she shook with the force of her orgasm. Long moments passed. She collapsed in a boneless heap against his broad chest.

Cinder moved her gently back until she reclined on the dashboard behind her. His hands moved down to her pussy. His fingers sank into the river of moisture that flowed from her, surrounding him, dripping onto the softly curling hairs of his pelvis. He parted her folds, spreading her so wide that the cool air caressed all of her tender secret flesh. His gaze bored into her there and he trembled against her.

The motions of his body had gentled so that now he only rocked into her as she reclined. Cinder leaned forward and let a glistening stream of saliva fall down onto their enjoined flesh. It sizzled as it splashed against them, so hot that it actually cooled in the pool of fiery wetness that swam there. Steffy cried out as it burned her, the sensation one of both pain and exquisite pleasure. His eyes met hers in smug challenge.

"I didn't scream," she said hoarsely, defensively.

"Not too far from it though, are you, love?" He smiled dangerously.

He flexed his cock deep within her and she came once more. He chuckled against her lips as she gasped and moaned. The heat of his hands stroked her from neck to knee, petting her over and over again, rewarding her for the endless intensity of her response to him.

When Steffy came down from her peak his fingers roughly tugged and rolled her nipples, effectively pushing her back up. Cinder undulated his hips against her, twisting his deeply buried cock. Disbelieving, she choked on a scream as she came again.

Her body felt like a swollen, aching puddle after her release subsided once again. Her senses were so heightened that just the moistness of Cinder's breath on her lips was a sexual torture. Shaking and weak she could only lay there as he once more renewed his assault upon her body. He knew her every erogenous zone, her every secret desire and used them as velvet edged weapons against her.

So much pleasure. Her teeth ached from it.

The tip of one of his fingers pressed into her clit, a lick of heat surged from him into her and she sobbed, coming again. But she would not scream. Cinder swore in defeat and slammed his lips and body against her. He thrust jarringly into her, bringing her, making her crazed with ecstasy and lust.

Liquid fire was the essence of his release as it flew from him into the condom. Steffy felt it burn against her as if there were no barriers between them. Her nails dug into his biceps, leaving bloody half-moons on his smooth, taut skin. Her head fell limply back as he gathered her closer against him once again.

"Fucking you is like reliving every wet dream I've ever had, all at once," he murmured against her throat.

"And riding you is like riding fire." She tried and failed to keep from bursting into laughter over her words. It was true, though, she had to admit it.

"You didn't scream." He sounded hurt and her gaze darted to his face. She saw nothing in his face to give away such pain, but wondered at what she'd heard there—for one small moment—in his voice.

Did he, maybe, love her a little?

She dare not ask herself yet if she loved him.

"Why do you want me to so badly?"

He didn't answer immediately, merely lifted her body off of him, pushed her back, and pulled his soiled condom off the still impressive length of his cock. The windows were so misted over that they couldn't see beyond them. He rolled his down and threw the condom out into the night. The chill of the air snuck in and danced on the sweat that moistened her body, cooling her considerably before Cinder rolled the window back up and blocked it away.

"I'd like to know that I can inspire such abandon from you. You're so self-contained, even when you're in the midst of your release." He seemed to consider his words carefully before continuing. "If you screamed I would know without a doubt that I have done my part in pleasuring you fully, so that all of your barriers were stripped away."

Steffy frowned. If she did that she would have no defenses against him. He would have mastered her then. How could she surrender so much when she never had before?

"I'm just not a screamer," she said with feigned lightness.

His eyes blazed into hers. "Every woman is a screamer with the right man."

She snorted. "What a sexist thing to say. Not all women scream."

"You will. You will scream for me one day."

Steffy said nothing. She crawled unsteadily back to her seat. At least she was no longer cold. The heat of the car had risen so that it resembled a greenhouse. It was difficult, but she managed to get her stockings and shoes back on in the confines of her seat.

With a startled shriek, Steffy jumped as there came a firm tapping at her window.

Chapter Ten

"So the Daemons have somehow mastered Traveling?" Cady exclaimed.

"I fear so. Zim and his team saw the group they fought tonight appear as if from nowhere. They're not so good as one of our Traveler Caste, but they are very dangerous with this new power at their disposal."

"I don't believe it. How can it be possible?" Obsidian was incredulous.

"The Daemons have many similarities to us. It was probably only a matter of time before they developed Caste traits," Tryton said wearily.

Obsidian, Cady, Edge and The Traveler sat in Tryton's personal apartments. Zim's unexpected news had brought them all together there for an emergency meeting to discuss their next step in controlling the Daemon threat.

"Why are they similar to us, Tryton?"

The blond-haired Elder started, clearly not expecting such a question. He darted a glance in The Traveler's direction and Cady wondered at the many secrets that no doubt passed between them.

"They just are, I suppose."

"Uh-uh, no way. I saw that look in your eyes. You know something and you're not telling." She pushed mercilessly. "Spill it."

Tryton sighed. "What I choose to share with you should be enough to satisfy. You don't need to know more than that, trust me."

"You know something about the Daemons that you're not telling us?" Obsidian asked with no small amount of shock. Cady thought it no doubt stemmed from the assumption that his leader had kept no secrets from him over the years. He was, after all, Tryton's most trusted warrior.

"I keep my own counsel when I wish. But I keep no secrets to myself that could serve to harm you," Tryton said firmly.

Tensions were high and rising by the second. Cady expertly steered them back away from the dangerous subject, feeling guilty that she'd been the cause for it in the first place. She knew she asked too many questions. But she was still human in the way she thought things through…she didn't always accept things blindly as the Shikars seemed wont to do. "So if these Daemons can Travel, what does that mean for us?"

"It means more danger for our warriors in the Territories." Tryton seemed as eager as she to let the talk of secrets fall silent once more. But Cady was no fool. She knew that a reckoning would come and soon. She only hoped that feelings weren't hurt when the time came for revelations.

"Only in the Territories? What about here? Can the Daemons come here?" Cady asked, thinking immediately of the safety of her infant son, Armand.

"No. We have strong wards here to protect us from such a threat. Ancient spells that will hold against any invasion. But the surface of this world is not so well guarded. And the dimensions that our Travelers frequent are at risk as well. Though the Daemons seem content enough to ravage the Earth and not those other ethereal plains."

"We are already spread thin in the Territories. We've lost several warriors over the past months and only a few days ago we lost an entire team in battle. What can we do to adequately meet and neutralize this new threat?" Obsidian sighed heavily.

"We may have to divide our teams up into smaller units," Tryton suggested.

"But that's suicide," Cady gasped.

"This war has grown too dangerous too quickly," Tryton muttered. "I must have time to think and confer with the Council. I knew no decisions could be made here between us tonight. I called this meeting simply to let you all know, my most loyal warriors, what it is you face now."

"We thank you, Elder," Obsidian said with great respect for his friend and leader.

"We'll have to bring Cinder back," Edge said, speaking for the first time since arriving.

"I know. And I think Steffy will have to come too. She's his woman now." Tryton smiled.

"I knew it!" Cady said excitedly. "They were too mean to each other not to be attracted."

"Only you would associate meanness with attraction, Cady," Obsidian said dryly.

"Shut up, Sid. You're just pissed because I told you so and you didn't believe me."

"I knew you were too much of a lady to rub it in," he countered.

Cady snorted.

"Is it possible that she could become a Shikar?"

"I don't know," Tryton said truthfully. "I'm not sure what made it possible for Cady to cross over into our world the way she did. We'll just have to wait and see."

"Perhaps our seed isn't poison to humans after all, but an elixir that can change them into our kind," Edge said thoughtfully.

"No." Tryton's voice was a thunderclap that echoed off the walls of the room. "Our seed is a poison to human women. Of that there can be no doubt."

"How do you know for certain?" Edge challenged softly.

"Once, long ago, a woman died in the arms of her Shikar lover. A direct result of lying with him. It was the first time such a tragedy had ever occurred. And over the years there have been others—thankfully only a few—to die. It's why the Council has forbidden unprotected sex between our species." Tryton's eyes were shadowed.

"What about sex between Shikar women and human men?" Cady asked curiously. She'd never heard anyone speak of such a thing.

Tryton and the Traveler both turned to her. She felt the weight of their stares bore heavily into her and wondered what is was she'd said to gain such a fierce reaction.

Tryton's words seemed guarded. Tentative. "There is no poison in a Shikar woman's embrace."

"Well, regardless, we have to retrieve Cinder soon. If Stefany wishes to come then the more the merrier, I say," Cady quipped.

Tryton nodded his agreement but the deep shadows never left his eyes. Cady wondered what knowledge or memory he held that put such a look into their depths. She doubted it would do her any good to ask. Tryton was good at keeping his own counsel.

But still…she couldn't help wondering.

* * * * *

Cady swirled her tongue over the thick crown of her husband's cock. Obsidian groaned against her pussy and bucked, pushing himself deeper into her mouth. She pumped him with her hands as she sucked and licked and nibbled. The heavy sac of his testicles she cupped lovingly in her hands, rolling and stroking them in the way she knew would best drive him wild.

He groaned and bucked against her again.

His mouth worked on her, licking, sucking and nuzzling her until she ached. His fingers squeezed and parted her buttocks. He licked the moue of her anus and she gasped around the thick flesh that filled her mouth. Obsidian had always been fascinated with her ass, loving it just as thoroughly as he did the rest of her.

She lifted her eyes to meet those black orbs that watched them from across the room. Grimm, gloriously naked, sprawled in his favored chair at the foot of the bed, stroking himself as he watched them. It wasn't often of late that their friend The Traveler had time to spend with them, seeking to have some small part of the love that stormed between them. Cady had, from the first, been both uncomfortable and titillated with his audience. But Grimm had never once taken liberties with her. He was content to watch them.

Grimm's eyes watched her every sucking movement on her husband's cock. She pulled back, determined to give him a good show, and licked the crown with dramatic sweeping motions of her tongue. She watched as Grimm squeezed his monstrously large cock and massaged his sac. She felt Obsidian's tongue lapping at her ass, felt his hands gently slapping her buttocks until they stung and no doubt glowed a rosy red.

Cady swallowed her husband's cock until he butted against the back of her throat. Obsidian's chin moved against her wet cunt. She rode his face. He rode hers. Grimm breathed heavily as he watched.

Cady felt the thick fullness of the *Smyl*—her favorite sex toy—as Obsidian slipped it into her pussy. The weighted balls that filled the *Smyl's* shaft vibrated inside of her. The toy swelled and conformed to the shape of her channel, filling her full to bursting as it trembled and shook inside of her. Obsidian's hands moved back to her ass cheeks, his tongue licking from where the *Smyl* filled her to her anus.

Cady moaned around Obsidian's cock. She was coming. She looked up into Grimm's eyes, to let him know how close she was to fulfillment. His shining black head fell back as he watched and his pumping hand increased its tempo. She bobbed her head faster up and down her husband's length.

They came in unison. The hot splash of Obsidian's sweet come flooded into her throat. She swallowed every delicious drop. Her pussy clenched violently around the *Smyl* and she came with a gush onto her husbands face. He licked her clean with relish and a hunger that only made her come harder. She saw the thick, creamy splash of Grimm's orgasm spurt up onto his belly before she closed her eyes against the force of her wondrous release.

Cady gave herself over to the addictive pleasure of her mate's wicked embrace. She didn't even notice when Grimm disappeared, leaving them as silently as he'd arrived.

Chapter Eleven

Cinder stiffened in the seat and the heat exuding from him increased exponentially. The bright glare of a flashlight illuminated the confines of the car and Cinder winced, his Shikar eyes overly sensitive to the artificial light.

Steffy rolled her window down and was, for once, happy to see the pea green of a *poleizi*—police—uniform.

"What's going on here?" the man asked politely, while obviously scanning the contents of her car. "Do you have your papers?"

Steffy quickly retrieved her I.D. and handed it to the officer, thankful that the policeman hadn't shown up ten minutes earlier. "Our car is out of fuel and my cell phone won't work out here." She glanced at the name on his badge. "Can you give us a lift to the nearest station, Officer Ehlers?"

"One moment, please." He went back to his car, where his partner was waiting, no doubt with the intention to enter her personal information into his computer, in search of any warrants or violations. She thanked her lucky stars that she had none—the policeman would have assumed all of the equipment filling the back of her car to be stolen otherwise.

A few minutes later the policeman appeared once more at her window and handed her papers back to her.

"We can call a tow truck for you, Fraulein Michanke but we are on patrol and cannot offer you a ride. I am sorry."

Police and their endless rules; how Steffy despised them. "A tow truck will cost me unnecessarily. I only need to refuel."

"I could call you a cab but I think very much that it would be just as costly all the way out here." He said this with a helpless, apologetic smile.

"Call this tow truck," Cinder commanded the policeman softly. "I'll pay for it."

Steffy sneered, knowing just how much money Tryton had given him to throw around. He wouldn't even notice the expense. But it was the principal of the thing—the waste of time and money and effort—that irked her so. She could well afford the price of a tow truck; she was very well paid for what she did for a living, but she was also notoriously tight-fisted with her money.

"If I gave you money and a petrol can, would you bring us the fuel so we can drive ourselves to the station?" she asked, grasping at straws.

"I am sorry, Fraulein. I would help you if I could, but my colleague and I must stay in this area unless we are called away from it. The petrol station, alas, is not in our assigned patrol area."

"Damn it." Stefany glared at him. "Fine, call the stupid tow truck."

Her look was lost on the police officer as an anguished scream sounded from his waiting vehicle. So much happened at once that Steffy's head swam. The policeman beside her drew his gun with a swift, fluid movement. Cinder's door flew open as he exited the vehicle. Another scream echoed, faded into a gurgle and then fell eerily silent.

"Stay in the car." The policeman's command fell on deaf ears as Cinder stepped from the car.

"Cinder, do as he says." Steffy grabbed for his hand and winced as her fingers burned from the heat of his skin. The policeman dashed off to investigate.

His head ducked back down into the car and his eyes glowed dangerously. "This is not good. Be on your guard and do exactly as I tell you."

"What's happening?" Her voice surprised her, steady as it sounded despite her sudden, overwhelming fear.

Cinder didn't answer her, merely looked back into the night, searching their surroundings intently. "Get out of the car, Stefany," he said, too softly, too gently.

"What's going on?"

"Get out of the damn car." His voice was a harsh whisper.

He couldn't have frightened her more if he'd roared the words at her.

She scrambled out of the car the same moment she heard several booming gunshots. The second policeman emitted a horrifying scream of terror and pain from the dark, enshrouding night. "Oh hell," she moaned helplessly.

Cinder was at her side immediately, dragging her into step beside him as he ran and crouched behind the car. "There's no ground cover for miles."

"Is that a good thing or a bad thing?" she asked, knowing even as she did so that she wouldn't like the answer.

"Could be either. It's good because I don't see any Daemons for leagues. It's bad because it means we can't hide from the ones that just killed those men."

"What makes you so sure it's Daemons out there?" she asked desperately.

"I can feel them," he murmured, all the while darting his eyes around, scanning their surroundings as if he feared an attack from any quarter, at any moment. He seemed to come to some decision after several seconds passed in silence. "You stay here. I'm going to try to draw them out into the open, away from that car. If you get in any trouble, scream for me."

"I will definitely scream for you," she said.

Cinder laughed shortly. "So it merely takes a Daemon to make you scream?"

"*Scheiße*," she breathed weakly. "Let it go, will you?"

He sobered and gave her a hard look from his glowing eyes. "I mean it. Stay here." And then he was gone.

Steffy's breath sobbed out of her as she crouched down behind the car. She hated feeling so exposed, wanted nothing more than to hop into her car and lock herself in. But she knew Cinder had wanted her out for a reason, out here where she would have a chance to flee if it came to that.

But flee to where? There was nothing but hills, the occasional cornfield, and pasture stretching out for miles around.

Golden firelight illuminated the night around her, startling her. Cinder had found the Daemons. The light dimmed and spots danced in her vision. Out of the corner of her eye she caught a glimpse of dark, hulking objects running across the median of the roadway with Cinder chasing behind them in immediate pursuit.

"Fuck this waiting crap," Steffy muttered and raced, full speed, to the still running cop car. Her well-trained eye immediately recognized the turbo charged e-class Mercedes' speed potential and found it to be more than satisfactory.

She almost tripped over a policeman's headless corpse.

"*Oh fucking hell*!" she cried out and immediately emptied the contents of her stomach onto the road at her feet. She'd lived a somewhat hard life, seen many horrible things...but she'd never seen a mutilated body before. In fact, she'd never seen a dead body before, period. "I'm sorry, mister. I'm so very, very sorry," she moaned piteously, knowing it was useless to apologize at this point, however heartfelt the sentiment.

Feeling the full weight of the situation upon her, knowing she was at least partly to blame for it—and all because of her stupid boredom and curiosity—she stepped past the body and jerked open the car's driver side door.

The other policeman—Officer Ehlers—was nowhere to be found. She tried not to think about what that might mean.

She slammed the door, gunned the engine—reveling in the rumbling purr that attested to the vehicle's power—and laid rubber as she streaked across the roadway. The car roared across the rough grass of the median with nary a complaint as she expertly steered it onto the same path Cinder and the Daemons had taken.

A black shape appeared in front of her and she screamed. Her headlights glinted off the slimy gore of the

Daemon's flesh. Instead of braking, as was her first instinct, she pushed the gas pedal to the floor. The car slammed into the monster, sending it flying up over the hood and away into the night. Steffy grunted but kept her foot on the gas.

She knew all too well by now that the Daemons couldn't be stopped so easily.

She saw a flame on the elbow of the opposite lane and raced to it. Leaning over, but careful to keep one hand on the wheel as she drove, she threw open the passenger door and slowed her speed.

"Hurry, Cinder. Get in!"

Cinder glanced back and did a double take upon seeing her in the car. He sent a lick of fire at the two Daemons before him and without even sparing them a second look to see if he'd damaged them, he dived into the car as she passed, slamming the door behind him. A Daemon appeared directly in front of them, but Steffy wasted no time in slowing or swerving the vehicle. She simply drove through the beast, launching him over the hood of the car and high into the air.

"I thought I told you to stay put."

"There were more than just those two. I hit one on the way over here. We're outnumbered and I, for one, don't want to wait around to find out just how many there are." Her words came fast and furious in her panic.

"By Grimm, how did the bastards get out here?"

"Don't ask me, you're the expert on all this scary shit."

"It was as if they just appeared. Out of nowhere," he murmured, as if speaking to himself.

"How do they usually come up here?"

"Through portals, holes in the Earth."

"Maybe there's one nearby." Her eyes scanned the roadway as she flew along it. Her mind wasn't really on the situation at hand. She was too busy panicking over the idea that she could get into trouble with the law if they were caught now. Two policemen lay dead, mutilated, along the road behind them and here they were speeding along in the dead men's patrol car.

No doubt about it, they were in some serious shit.

"It doesn't feel that way to me. I'm not a Hunter like Cady but I can feel the Daemons when they're close and it felt to me like...but that would be impossible."

"What? What would be impossible?" Her voice rose along with her alarm.

"Cady said their presence ebbed and flowed that first night we were in Hamburg. And tonight it was the same when I felt them. Like they were there one minute and gone the next. Almost like they were Traveling."

"So what are you saying? That these things can just appear whenever, wherever they want to?"

"They didn't feel strong enough for that. And I just can't believe they can Travel... Grimm help us, but that's what it felt like."

"Oh fuck me." The car's engine purred more loudly as she increased her speed. Her hands sweated nervously on the wheel.

The car swallowed the miles easily, effortlessly.

Cinder glanced back behind them. He turned around. Then glanced back once more.

"What is it?"

"Nothing."

Several minutes passed. Cinder kept glancing back behind them.

"How fast can this car go?" he asked, suddenly.

"Pretty fast," she said weakly. "Why?"

"Go a little faster," he said gently. Calmly.

Too calmly.

"Why?" Her voice was nearly a shriek.

His eyes burned into hers, glowing fiercely. The lights from the instrument panel glittered eerily over his face. "Something's coming. Something big."

Steffy groaned and stomped the pedal to the floor.

Chapter Twelve

The ground shuddered and quaked, and the car would have swerved if not for her iron control upon the wheel.

"What was that?" Her voice was hoarse with the effort it took to keep from screaming.

"We must go faster," he growled in response, darting quick, furtive glances behind them.

"I'm going 160 kilometers an hour!"

"That's not nearly fast enough."

"Oh God." She increased her speed until the speedometer read 185 kph—roughly 115 miles per hour.

The ground trembled again.

Steffy looked up into the rearview mirror. "Ohmygodohmygodohmygod!"

"Don't look back!"

But it was too late. She'd seen it. The giant...*thing*...that was causing the asphalt behind them to erupt like a geyser. Whatever it was, it was huge. Massive. And it was tunneling through the ground, hot and heavy on their trail despite their speed.

Cinder grabbed for the mounted shotgun that was locked to the dash. A long, glowing red blade shot out from his index finger, cutting through the lock as though it were butter. The smell of burning metal permeated their surroundings.

Steffy jerked the wheel in surprise. The car swerved dangerously on the shaking ground before she expertly righted it. "What *is* that thing?"

He held his hand up and the glowing blade retreated back into his flesh. "One of my foils. I don't use them very often."

"Foils?" she asked weakly. What the hell were foils?

"I'll explain later," he promised impatiently. "Just drive." He aimed the shotgun between their seats.

"Duck. This is going to be loud," was all the warning he gave her before he fired.

The rear windshield exploded violently.

Steffy's ears rang and her head swam dizzyingly. She held control of the car but only barely. Cinder leaned farther back over their seats, pumped the shotgun, and fired again. And again. He fired until Steffy lost count, her ears deafened by the noise, then turned back around. "Damn it, woman, go faster!"

"I'm going as fast as this damn car will go," she shouted.

"Holy Horde," he growled and shoved his foot down over hers where it rested on the gas pedal.

"Oh yeah, like that's going to help! I've already got it floored." The car rocked dangerously as the pavement around them surged. "Move your fucking foot back!"

Cinder pulled back and Steffy heard the swell of the music in her head reach an alarming crescendo. She needed to think. Needed to come up with a plan to outmaneuver the thing that was gaining on them. She let her instincts take over, trusted in the precognitive sense she desperately hoped was there as Tryton had told her, and felt her fear leave almost at once.

"Hang on," she gritted out.

She threw the car into neutral, took her foot off the gas and yanked up the emergency brake. The car flew into the controlled spin Steffy had orchestrated, turning at an almost 90-degree angle onto a blind drive that led into a cornfield away from the main roadway. She disengaged the emergency brake—had only needed it to help her bank the turn—popped the shifter into a lower gear for better traction and floored the gas pedal once more.

"Shit. I didn't even see this road," Cinder rumbled in surprise.

"Me either," she admitted.

Cinder stared at her in something akin to surprise. Steffy ignored him, tearing through the narrow, rough-hewn path that could hardly be called a road.

"Have we lost them?" She asked.

Cinder stared behind them. "I don't see them."

"*Scheiße*!" Steffy screamed and yanked the wheel sharply to the right. The thing had somehow appeared no more than a few yards in front of them. She'd only barely had enough time to react after catching sight of the monstrosity.

"They *are* Traveling!" Cinder roared.

The car lurched and bounced alarmingly as they drove over endless, towering stalks of corn. The engine whirred and screeched as the vegetation choked off its intake of air. The wheel shuddered dangerously in her hands.

"Cinder." Steffy breathed his name, instinctively sensing what was about to happen.

"What?" he said, growing still, as if he too knew what was coming.

"I'm sorry I didn't scream for you." A strange calm had enveloped her.

"I won't let us die like this," he said, his voice already sounding far away to her ears.

"You should know I love you," she admitted, knowing it was the truth and realizing that now—of all times—it mattered more than anything that she let him hear how she felt.

The car bounced, went airborne over a hidden dip in the ground, flipped and rolled three times. The screaming sound of ripping metal and shattering glass filled the air with a symphony of sound, which mixed and replayed for endless moments along with the music in Steffy's racing mind. Pain lanced throughout her extremities. Blood streamed into her eyes. The car rolled once more then settled, almost gently, on its side.

Then all was still. And there was silence in the night once more.

Chapter Thirteen

"Stefany. Damn it, Steffy, wake up."

But she didn't want to wake up. For with awareness would come pain, and she'd had more than her share over the years. She didn't need or want any more now. She moaned and sought the blessed darkness once more.

"Wake up." Hands were pulling her, tugging her out of the wreckage.

Her eyes felt sticky as she struggled to open them. The salty sting of blood blurred her vision and caused her to wince. Her lips were swollen, split open and aching, but she spoke over the pain. "Are you okay?" she croaked. Even her throat felt bruised.

A glowing red foil streaked out and cut her free of the seat belt, which still held her trapped in the mangled car. "I'm fine. I've already healed myself. It's you I'm worried about." He pulled her free, put one arm at her back, another beneath her bent knees, and lifted her against him.

He ran with her, deeper into the dense field of corn.

"Where are the Daemons?" Her tone sounded dreamy and drugged even to her ears. Everything felt oddly surreal to her now.

He lowered her gently onto the ground. His hands swept over her, checking her for injuries and filling her with heat, easing away some of her aches. "You've got some cracked ribs and a dislocated shoulder, I think. Your head is bleeding. Shit, you're bleeding all over." His voice shook around his stubbornly clenched teeth.

"Where are the Daemons?" she repeated.

His eyes glowed down into hers. He winced upon seeing the cuts and bruises that marred her face. "I don't know," he admitted in a growl.

They fell silent, listening for their foes.

"Get out of here before they come back," Steffy said softly, looking at his worried face in the shadows.

"You're stupid if you think I'll just leave you here." He pulled back angrily and avoided looking at her injured form.

"Cinder."

His eyes met hers once more.

"Go. Please go. I need to… I need to…" she coughed, and blood sprayed in a mist down her chin. "I need to know you're safe," she ended in a wheeze. The pain that swallowed her body intensified and she couldn't be sure if that was a good thing or a bad thing. Good because it could mean she was alive enough to still feel…bad because it could mean she wouldn't be alive for very long.

"No. I'm not leaving you," he gritted out, running his hands over her once more. The heat he left behind lingered then fled as her form rejected it. Her body didn't need that heat, it seemed.

Her body was already beginning to shut down, going into shock.

The ground shuddered beneath them, drawing their attention. "They're coming," she whispered.

"They have a Canker-Worm with them."

She was too weak to ask what the hell a Canker-Worm was. "Go. Get out of here."

"No." He dragged her up, made her gain her feet though she teetered drunkenly. "We'll face them together."

He half dragged, half carried her deeper into the field. "I'm hurt, Cin. I'll only slow you down. Leave me here. I'm so tired," she moaned.

Cinder said nothing, only clutched her tighter to him and hurried their pace. The ground roiled, sent them stumbling, but he merely righted them and kept going.

"We can't outrun them."

"I know," he said simply.

They had made it no farther than the middle of the vast field before a giant, towering creature exploded out of the ground in front of them, sending great chunks of earth flying high into the sky as it came.

Steffy was too weak to do anything but tremble as her eyes took in the horror before them.

The Canker-Worm rose out of the ground, its body measuring at least thirty feet in diameter. Its length above the surface was fifteen feet if it was an inch, and there was no guessing how much more of its body lie below ground. It was shaped like an earthworm, tube-like and limbless, but there the resemblance ended. Its head was split into two parts and the gaping maws of its mouths were filled with brown fangs the length of Steffy's body.

Its body was brownish black—muddy colored—and its flesh seemed a mixture of both rough scales and slime. Oozing boils steamed and ran with yellow pus all over its form, burning the ground as it wept down. The smell of rotten carrion filled the air, and Steffy, beyond pain or fear or reason, gagged as the stench filled her nose and mouth with its rancid warmth.

A large Daemon sat atop the worm, as a human would sit atop a horse.

Steffy could have sworn that she heard and felt the heavy pounding rhythm of the Daemon's heart.

Boom. Boom. Boom.

It echoed in perfect rhythm with the tempo playing out in her mind.

"Don't look, Steffy." Cinder pulled her tighter to him, pulling her head down to his chest in a protective gesture.

And Steffy was too tired, too frightened, to do anything but let him. She knew they were going to die.

"*Eprish 'ald Horde, primarsandh*!" came the Daemon's war cry, and his voice held the suffering of a thousand damned souls, the evil of a million black hearts. His was the wrath of the endless army—the Horde itself.

The last vestiges of strength fled Steffy in the face of such dark hatred. She sagged heavily against Cinder, falling to her knees even as she clutched her arms around his waist in an effort to remain standing.

But Cinder remained standing. As strong and fierce as always, ever the proud Shikar warrior in the midst of his enemies. Daemons moved to flank them, surrounding them, and Cinder didn't even flinch. He faced the Daemons and the monstrous Horde Worm as casually and coolly as he might go to a dinner party.

If Steffy hadn't been in the midst of a storm of pain and fear she would have smiled at the sight.

"Give Steffy to us and we will end you quickly."

Steffy choked on a cry of pure terror. Hearing her name on the putrid lips of the Daemon atop the Worm made her heart stop dead in her chest before it resumed its thunderous, stuttering pace. *How had that monster known her name*?

"Why do you want her?"

"Give her to us! *Arr'chen shidd 'ald Horde.* Do not invoke our wrath."

"Come and get her if you think you've got the courage," Cinder challenged arrogantly.

The ground rolled. The Worm's charge was held in check at the last moment by the Daemon atop it…but only just.

"You will die, Shikar." Shadows oozed over Steffy's brain as the monster's hellish voice stabbed through her ears.

"After you."

Steffy cringed and clutched at Cinder, knowing there was such a thing as too much bravado. He looked down at her as the Daemons around them began to inexorably close in. His eyes burned and a halo of heat surrounded them.

"Hold on, baby. Hold on tight."

There was an intense surge of heat. It ate at her eyeballs and mouth. She closed both and buried her face against his thigh as she knelt there on the ground. More heat swallowed them, rolling from Cinder to her and beyond.

The Daemons lunged with a mighty cry.

The ground around the Canker-Worm roiled and belched as it charged.

Behind her clenched lids, Steffy saw a bright orange glow flicker and pulse and grow.

Then came the swell of agonizing heat. The roar of flame. The crackling sound of burning vegetation. And the scream of many dying things.

Steffy opened her eyes, but the heat and the light engulfed her.

And she was swallowed in flames as Cinder's power exploded in a blaze that ate the world.

* * * * *

Long minutes—perhaps hours—later, Steffy opened her eyes and watched the spots that danced before her vision. Her hands were hurting from having clutched Cinder so tightly and so long. Cinder was breathing hard, but otherwise seemed none the worse for wear. The smell of burning hair filled her nostrils and she saw that the ends of her hair had been singed away.

But other than that she too appeared unharmed by Cinder's flames.

The Daemons, however, had not been so lucky.

In fact, they—along with the Canker-Worm—had disappeared entirely. Burnt to ash. Along with several hundred yards of the cornfield. Steffy gasped to see the extent of the damage Cinder had caused to their surroundings. They stood in the middle of a massive black, charred circle. Smoke still rose in lazy wisps from still flaming stalks of corn dotted about the field.

Cinder had succeeded in devastating several acres of land. He'd laid waste to them with the explosion of his power.

"*Scheiße,*" she said weakly, looking around them in wonder.

"By Grimm…" he said shakily, "did I actually *do* that?" Steffy saw his eyes were wide with his own shock.

"Didn't you mean to do that?" she cried, not a little unnerved by his obvious surprise.

"I've never," he took a deep breath, "done anything like that. I didn't know I could."

"*Scheiße.*"

Cinder tore his eyes away from the burnt field with an expression that looked almost like horror. Steffy found no comfort in knowing that he'd been just as surprised as she at the results of his release of control. Not that she was ungrateful for those results—they were alive, weren't they? But it was still daunting to know that Cinder hadn't, himself, been aware of his own strength and power.

His eyes met hers and immediately refocused on their situation. "Come on. We have to get out of here. And you need medical attention."

"Fuck. How the hell am I going to explain all this to a doctor?" She laughed…and lapsed into deep, racking coughs as a result.

Her heart and mind quailed as she saw the bright red blood that stained her hands.

Chapter Fourteen

"Don't you close your eyes, damn it! Stay with me." Cinder dragged her roughly along with him as he raced up to the old truck parked negligently in the quaint farmhouse's tiny graveled driveway.

"I'm so tired," she whispered. "Let me rest."

"If you sleep now you won't wake up," he said with brutal frankness. He looked at her pale face as she tried to lean against him and rest. He gritted his teeth around a surge of panic. She wasn't going to make it.

She *would* make it, he vowed. He would force her to live if he had to.

"We've been walking for hours," she moaned piteously.

"Only an hour. We're lucky this place wasn't farther away." He sidled up to the truck.

"You can't drive. I'll have to." He only hoped it wasn't too hard a skill to master or they were both screwed. Dawn would be on the rise within the next two hours.

"I hope this hunk of junk is an automatic then," she muttered.

Cinder tried the door. It was locked. He cursed blackly, shook Steffy as she tried to nod off—he'd been shaking her awake more and more often over the course of the past hour—and smashed the window in with his fist. As swiftly as he could he unlocked the door, yanked it open and shoved Steffy inside. He followed her, looking around warily to assure himself that no one had heard the noise.

"How do I turn it on?"

"Look under the visors. There might be a spare set of keys, though I doubt it." Steffy was visibly struggling to help him as much as she could. The bruises and cuts that covered her face and body were an alarmingly stark contrast to the chalky pallor of her skin.

And, of course, there weren't any spare keys to be found.

"Hang on," Steffy said and drunkenly leaned down to the floorboard at Cinder's feet. She fiddled unsteadily with some wires down there and within minutes the truck's engine roared to life. Steffy leaned back with a bleary smile. "I used to be able to hotwire a brand new car in less than a minute. I must be slipping." She sighed and leaned heavily back in her seat.

The door of the farmhouse flew open and a man in his bedclothes came running out into the drive, waving his hands and yelling.

"Shit. How do I do this?" Cinder growled.

Steffy leaned over and pulled the stick that protruded out from the steering. "That's reverse. Hit the gas, that pedal there," she motioned weakly, "and back up into the road."

Somehow Cinder managed to do it, tires throwing gravel at the angry farmer as he sped backwards. He slammed on the brakes as he hit the pavement of the road, jerking the vehicle brutally. Steffy reached over and repositioned the stick.

"That's drive. That's all you need to know." She smiled encouragingly at him, but it was ruined as her lip cracked and began once more to bleed.

Cinder stomped on the gas and off they sped down the road. It was unsteady going at first as he became accustomed to the nuances of steering the vehicle, but at last they were easily eating up the miles, on their way back to the city.

"Don't go to sleep," became Cinder's litany as the minutes crawled by. He was forced to shake her several times here and there to punctuate his command.

Steffy's cough got increasingly worse.

"I think my lungs are fucked up," she said thickly, and by the tone of her voice Cinder knew she wasn't really aware of much. Shock had set in. Everything had probably taken on a surreal, dreamlike quality to her. She was beyond fear. Beyond pain.

It wasn't a good sign.

She coughed again and it sounded wet. Bubbly. Thick.

"You'll be fine," he gritted out as if just saying it would make it so. "Just stay awake. Stay with me."

He reached across the seat and grabbed her hand in one of his. His heart stuttered at the cold feel of that small hand swallowed up in the heat of his. The fire that hovered beneath his skin moved to embrace her, to shield her in heat. He pushed his power out and over her, fearing what her increasing coldness might mean.

He couldn't lose her. He'd rather die a thousand deaths than be without her for one single moment.

"Did I tell you about the first time I used my Incinerator ability?" he asked, knowing full well he hadn't. He'd been stingy with her, refusing to share much of his past with her. But no more. He would share with her now, and gladly.

Hopefully he'd have a lifetime to share with her.

Steffy's eyes were glazed as she looked at him, but he could see the curiosity swimming in their depths as well as the pain. He saw that curiosity as a good sign. A sign to show she was still with him. It would have to do for the moment.

"I was nine years old. I was with my aunt, Desondra—"

"Desondra is your aunt?" she asked, obviously surprised.

"Yes." He was pleased to see a little bit of awareness return to her. "She was always totally cool—as Cady would so blithely put it. I liked spending time with her. Anyway, I was with Desondra when it happened. My mother was a Council member and my father was out guarding the Gates. Desondra and I were making tents out of bed sheets in her sitting room—"

Steffy laughed. "I did that when I was little, too."

"And we were crawling around beneath them when all of a sudden the sheets just went up in flames. I remember my skin felt so itchy and swollen and hot and then—*Poof*!—there were flames all around me."

"What did you do?"

"Well, I freaked out," he admitted. "My father had sensed that I would be an Incinerator but I never really gave any thought to it, so I was more than a little surprised when it happened." He'd never shared the embarrassing tale with anyone—Desondra had always been the one to torture him with the telling. "I screamed like a little girl and starting beating at the flames. But when I did that, flames shot out of my hands and the fire just got worse. Desondra was caught in the middle. Her hair singed completely away until there was only stubble left, but other than that the flames didn't seem to hurt her. I didn't know it then, but she was protected from the fire mostly because I had enough control over the fire's magic to keep her safe. I'm thankful for that now." He thought of the earlier explosion of fire and was doubly thankful that Steffy hadn't been hurt by his loss of control.

He'd been just as shocked as she by the results of his unleashed power.

And to think, he hadn't even completely let go of his tight hold on control. He shuddered to think what might happen if he ever gave in and tested the full extent of his power. Tryton had been at him for years to attempt such a thing…but he had refused such an experiment. Quite simply, he didn't want to know what he was capable of.

"How did you put the fire out?"

"Tryton came bursting through the room, raised his arms, and a rain shower appeared over our heads and put out the flames. Desondra and I sat in a mess of water and charred sheets looking like a couple of drowned rats. I thought for sure I was in deep shit, but after a few minutes Tryton burst into laughter. It was the first time I'd ever seen him laugh. I didn't know what to think."

Steffy smiled but he was glad that she refrained from laughing. He couldn't bear the sound of her coughing just then.

"Desondra didn't speak to me for a whole month, but once her hair started growing back she forgave me. And in the meantime, Tryton had me training under one of the Incinerators so that I could learn a little control over my power. Dear Desondra loves to tell the story at gatherings, just to embarrass me. She forgave me, but she didn't forget."

"You had a good childhood," Steffy said with a gentle grin.

Cinder gritted his teeth at the memory of her words regarding her own childhood. When the danger to them was passed…he'd be visiting her father. Not that he'd be telling her his intentions. He doubted she'd want to hear the details of what he would do to the bastard. Or approve of them.

Better to keep that black business to himself. And The Traveler who would, no doubt, help him locate the man when the time came.

"The best. We Shikars take care of our own. Our families are the most important thing to us."

"And after family comes the safety of mankind."

"Yes." He'd never seen it as so noble an endeavor, but when she said it that way it made his heart swell with pride.

"What about your parents? Tell me about them."

"They passed from the living world. Together, as it was meant to be. When I was fifty. A long while ago…though I miss them still."

They were silent for long moments. The city loomed ahead. Steffy looked over at him and his heart quailed at what he saw there.

"I'm dying, Cin," she said simply.

"No," he ground out harshly. "No you're not. I won't let you."

"Something's broken inside me. But it doesn't hurt." She seemed compelled to reassure him of that. "It's okay."

"You'll be fine..." His voice broke. He tightened his fingers on the steering wheel and sped the truck up. "We'll get you to a healer."

"No. No doctors. No hospitals. I don't want to die in a strange place. Take me home."

"I can't heal you, Steffy. I haven't the skill. You need a healer."

"No doctor can help me." The words were spoken with a gentle finality.

"I won't let you die," he choked out. "Just hold on until I can get you to a clinic or something."

"Don't be sad, Cin. It's not your fault. It's mine. I shouldn't have gone out tonight. It was stupid. Sorry."

"And you can be sure that I'll spank you silly for that once you're better. But I promise you'll like it...if you'll just hold on for me now."

"I like you a lot, Cinder. You're very cool." She breathed a gentle laugh. "You need to know that. Don't feel bad for me, 'kay?" She coughed a little. Weakly. "Take me home," she sighed.

He would take her home. How could he not? He knew, though he refused to accept it, that she was just too hurt for any human healer to help her.

Ten minutes later he was carrying her up the stairs to her apartment. Bloody coughs wracked her frame until she trembled. But there was nothing for either of them to do. Cinder sent comforting warmth into her, hoping it could help to lessen some of her pain, fighting against tears of hopelessness that threatened to unman him.

He kicked open the door to her home and nearly dropped her in surprise.

The Traveler reached out to both of them, laying his hands with gentle care on Steffy's brow, and took them home.

Chapter Fifteen

Cinder paced the length of his bedroom for what must have been the ten thousandth time. He glanced into the mirror that stood against the wall before his bed, taking in the scene behind him with a wince. Steffy seemed so small in his massive bed. It didn't help that two tall Shikars towered over her as she lay there.

"Why is it taking so long?" he muttered.

"It's taking both Obsidian's skills and Agate's to do this. She's pretty banged up," Cady said gently.

It had been well over an hour since The Traveler had brought them here before going to retrieve their most talented healers—Obsidian and Agate. How The Traveler had known to come for them in that moment, Cinder hadn't asked. He wasn't sure he wanted to know. The idea of The Traveler having such a strong connection to him or Steffy was an alarming one.

The Traveler was too powerful for his own good and it made Cinder uneasy at the best of times.

Obsidian's hand on his shoulder startled him. He'd been too occupied with his own thoughts to notice his friend coming upon him. That had never happened before and was telling to just how much Steffy's well being had come to matter to him.

The sorrow in Obsidian's eyes sent a shard of ice through his heart. He didn't want to hear what his friend had to say.

"We can't help her," Obsidian whispered.

"No. You have to help her," Cinder gritted out.

"We've tried, Agate and I both. But her body is human…humans are frail, tender creatures. You know that. Their bodies don't repair themselves as easily as ours do. I'm sorry."

Cinder reached out and grabbed Obsidian's shirt by the laces at his throat. "Get back over there and help her, damn it."

Obsidian's eyes glittered dangerously. "If you weren't my friend, I would kick your ass for so much as touching me in anger," he said softly.

Cady rushed to separate them. "Cinder didn't mean any offense, hon. Let it go."

"I am sorry, my friend. Her human body is too wounded to heal. I am sorry." Obsidian's voice had gentled once more.

Cinder choked and was startled to feel the fiery burn of his tears sizzle down his cheeks. "There has to be something…she can't just die. Not like this. Not now."

The Traveler appeared quietly, stealthily beside them. Like a ghost. "There might be a slight chance to save her, still." His face, as always, was shrouded in the black cowl he wore, but Cinder could have sworn he saw something there. Something he'd never expected to see in his life.

"*Grimm*?" he whispered, beyond shock.

The Traveler took a swift step back, distancing himself from Cinder's discovery. But Cinder knew—simply knew—that he was standing in the presence of a legend. The Traveler was Grimm…and had been all along. Did Tryton know? Of course he had to, it was no doubt why he conferred so closely with The Traveler. But why keep his identity a secret?

He pulled himself away from the shocking revelation and focused on the moment at hand. "What can be done to save her? I'll do everything I can to help."

"It isn't up to you, Cinder," The Traveler said in his beautiful, dark voice. "The choice will be Steffy's."

"You mean to bring her over? To make her one of us?" Cady breathed in wonder, realizing what Grimm intended before the others could grasp the situation.

"Well, Cinder will do the honors, of course." Grimm said dryly. "But I will be here to try and keep her safe. And of course, I won't do anything if Steffy decides not to choose this path."

"But I'll have to lay with her to bring her over," Cinder said, shocked at the idea. "She's too injured for such a thing."

"If she chooses to do this, I can keep her pain from her. She will feel only pleasure. I will let no harm come to her."

"I can't do that. I can't be with her while she's hurt..."

"Then she will die." Grimm said it as calmly as he might have said the sky was blue.

"Don't you say that, damn you! Don't talk about her as if her life were unimportant."

"She's just a human. When she dies a hundred more will be born to take her place."

Cinder didn't stop to think at how pointedly goading, how deliberately insulting Grimm's words were.

"She's not just any human, you son of a bitch. She's my woman! And I won't let her die. I can't."

"Then you'll do what must be done to save her."

"Yes, damn you. I'll do it. I'd do anything to save her."

"Leave us," The Traveler commanded the others in the room. Within moments, Cinder and Steffy were alone with Grimm, the legend.

He walked over to the bed and sat beside Steffy upon it. He tucked a wild tangle of pink hair back over her brow. "If we can bring her over to us, her body will still need to be healed of its physical wounds. Her Shikar body will be easily repaired by Obsidian or Agate. But…already she walks in shadow, hand-in-hand with Death. We haven't much time to save her. "

Cinder joined him and almost cried out at the look of pale death on Steffy's face. "Hurry, then."

"I will do what I can, just as you will. But Cinder." Grimm pulled the cowl back down from his face, revealing the star-lit black eyes—Traveler eyes—that seemed able to look down into Cinder's soul and uncover every hidden secret that lay there. "I can promise you nothing. Do you understand? Even I am not sure what will come of what we do here."

In other words, they were flying by the seat of their pants.

"Thank you. For trying." It took a lot of effort to get the words past his numb lips.

The Traveler bent down by Steffy's ear and began to whisper words that Cinder could not hear. And even if he could he probably wouldn't have understood the most ancient and primitive tongue of his own people.

Words that were several thousand years old.

As old as Grimm himself.

* * * * *

"Would you live, Steffy? Would you live as one of us?" The words were in a tongue she didn't recognize…but her soul understood them and that was the most important thing, she supposed.

"I'm tired." She spoke the only truth she really knew.

"I know. You are dying. But you can live if you wish it. Not as a human but as a Shikar."

"I'm not a Shikar."

"You can be, if you but wish it."

"How?" Hope was something she was too weak, too tired to feel. But it was there, all the same, waiting for her to rally her will enough to grasp it.

"Cinder's seed can change you. Can bring you over into our world."

"His seed?"

"His sperm. He could lay with you now, could make love to you now, and you would have a chance at a new life."

"But I'm hurt. I can't…"

"You can. And you will feel pleasure. I'll see to that, if you'll trust me."

"I don't want to die." She admitted it freely, knowing that the man who spoke to her in so beautiful a voice would never see the admission as a sign of weakness or cowardice.

"Then I will do all that is within my power to keep you alive. But you may hate me for saving you, eventually."

"No. I won't hate you. I could never hate you." His voice wrapped her up in soothing comfort. How could she ever hate the owner of such a magical voice? How could she do anything but trust and love and revere such a being?

"I hope you speak the truth, little one. Now lie back and feel no more pain. No pain, only pleasure."

No pain…no pain…no pain. The words whispered through her mind over and over again until there was no pain. Only a tranquil darkness that ate at the cruel edges of the world, keeping her safe from harm. Safe from death.

* * * * *

Grimm's black eyes met Cinder's. "She will feel only the pleasure of your embrace. But I must stay and hold her spirit anchored within her body or we'll lose her." He rose and positioned himself behind the head of the bed. He dipped one finger into the blood that still seeped from the many wounds on her body and raised it to his lips. He inhaled the scent deeply, licked the essence of her lifeblood from his fingers and looked to Cinder. "I have her scent; she will not escape us. I won't let her escape us." He cupped his hands around Steffy's head, was silent for a long moment, then looked up at Cinder and nodded his head.

"It is time. Her life is in your hands now, my friend."

Chapter Sixteen

Cinder's hand's shook as they cupped her breasts. She hadn't even noticed when he'd taken her clothes off. Had she been asleep? She felt weighty, dreamy. Out of touch with reality. Perhaps she had slept.

"Nervous?" she asked him, teasing.

His eyes shot up to hers and held something that looked like surprise. "Aren't you?"

"No, silly. Though I guess you're virile enough to unnerve me." She laughed softly and was pleased with how seductive it sounded, even to her ears. "At least a little."

Cinder looked up over her head as if he saw something there. She followed his gaze above the bed but saw only shadows. They were in his room, in his Shikar home. She wondered for a lazy moment how they'd gotten there, but the thought slid over her mind before it could take hold of anything. It didn't matter how they'd come, only that they were together.

"What are you looking at?" she asked, stroking her hands down the rippling muscles of his chest and stomach.

"Can't you…can't you see?"

"See what?" She laughed. "What's wrong, silly?"

His eyes roved over her features, as if it were the last time he'd ever see her face. "Nothing. Nothing's wrong."

His words sounded like a lie…but try as she might she couldn't wonder why. Her mind seemed content to wander away from such a potentially dangerous topic, focusing instead on Cinder's nude body as it glistened and burned over hers.

His lips whispered over her brow, searing her where they touched until she was squirming with growing arousal. It seemed forever that he pressed light, gentle kisses over her face and neck before settling at last on her mouth. He tasted heavenly to her starving lips. It seemed an age had passed since their last kiss.

And he was so gentle!

Cinder was never one for gentleness. Had always been a rough and demanding lover in her bed. But now he held her with such fierce tenderness that it brought tears to her eyes. He seemed to cherish each kiss, each caress, as if determined to let her know how precious she was to him. Oh, how deeply she loved him for it.

And she knew without a doubt that she would love him forever.

His hands were like the brush of a warm wind over the curves and slopes of her body. Her skin tingled deliciously. Her nipples tightened and swelled as his palms slid over her in long, sweeping strokes. He was petting her from head to toe, starting with her hair and ending with massaging strokes at the soles of her feet. Before long, as she sighed and stretched beneath his magical hands, he seemed to grow easier, less desperately tender in his loving.

His hair was a cool shock to her fevered flesh when he bent his head close enough for her to feel it. The stabbing pebble of her nipple slipped against his hot lips when she arched up against him. Her fingers kneaded into the broad expanse of his shoulders, squeezing and testing the resilience of his tightly muscled flesh.

"You're so damn sexy," she moaned.

His eyes twinkled down into hers and a boyish grin split the overly serious contours of his face. "You're pretty sexy yourself…I *guess*," he teased.

She leaned up and bit his lip lightly as punishment. "You guess?" she said with a feigned pout. Shamelessly she rubbed the hot mound of her sex against the hard rise of his.

"No. Not sexy. More than that."

"What then?" she coaxed.

"Severely, deliciously fuckable," he growled, and took her lips in a deep kiss, licking against her tongue with his.

The giggle that bubbled from her mouth into his blurred into a moan as his fingers rolled one of her nipples between them with stunning expertise. He was a magician when it came to her body. He seemed to know exactly what she liked, when she would like it, and just how much of it she could take before exploding into a thousand points of light.

Her knees fell wide apart and he settled between them easily. She was so wet that his cock slipped and slid against her as he moved, sliding his lips from her mouth to her jaw to her neck. Undulating up against him, she gasped with rising, aching pleasure. Her hands flew over the planes of his back, even as he nearly burned her with the amount of heat he was giving off.

He licked one of her nipples with the flat of his tongue. His head moved so that he could repeat the decadent caress over the other. With a masculine, predatory growl he took her whole breast in his mouth and suckled mercilessly. The fingers of one hand pinched and tugged at her free nipple as he sucked her, so that it wouldn't feel neglected, while his other hand held his weight up off of her with an effortless show of strength.

His mouth left her breast to glisten and cool in the air as he trailed wet, hot kisses to her ribcage and stomach. His tongue delved into her navel, sending jolts of heat into her with each flick of that devilish appendage. His hand trailed down between her thighs and teased the seam of her cunt until she parted her legs even wider to him. He chuckled triumphantly and nipped her navel in reward, licking and kissing and nibbling her until she keened with wild pleasure.

And those wicked, knowing fingers of his traced the swollen lips of her sex, toying with her labia piercing until she was certain her juices flooded down onto the mattress beneath her. She was so hot. So aroused. If he didn't take her soon she was going to scream.

And wouldn't that make him happy?

"Please," she moaned.

"Please what?" He murmured the question into the swell of her tummy and it rumbled through her, the feel of his voice a caress all its own.

"Fuck me." She strained upwards, pushing her wet sex towards him wantonly.

"I won't fuck you, but I'll make love to you," he said, eyes playfully twinkling up from his position between her thighs.

"Make love to me then," she commanded with a smile and bucked against him.

"You're so wet," he whispered, dipping one lone finger into her moisture.

She moaned and writhed again.

"How can you be so wet…like this…at a time like this?"

That indefinable and troubling *something*, which kept trying to intrude in on her dreaming thoughts, was there, naked, in his voice. She pushed it away, vowing that nothing would ruin this magical time with him. Here in his arms nothing mattered but that they love each other.

"I love you, Cin," she breathed, feeling compelled to tell him.

"I love you too, baby," he shocked her by replying.

His finger stroked her once more before he rose up between her legs and positioned his cock at her portal. He was unprotected, naked and velvety and dusky smooth without his condom. She wondered at that anomaly and for a moment unknowingly teetered on the brink of a frightening realization. But as Cinder smoothly entered her in one long thrust she cried out and let him take her into oblivion.

He stretched her. Moved into her like a storm of fire and flame. His thumb stroked and rolled her clit, smearing her wetness onto the swollen flesh so that it glided easily. Silkily. He thrust in and out of her, so tightly filling her that she thought perhaps they were well and truly one being in those moments when he reached for the very heart of her.

"Oh, Cinder," she breathed and moaned in a litany.

"I would do anything for you. Do anything to keep you with me. I will always love you, Steffy. Always," he whispered fervently into her mouth as he lowered himself slowly onto her and kissed her.

He was so hard inside of her. So thick and long and strong. But he moved so gently inside of her that she wept with the beauty of it all. With each down stroke he made Steffy clutch him to her with desperate, loving hands. She wrapped her legs around his waist, locked her ankles upon the pumping slope of his buttocks. His arms were braced on either side of her head, his hands holding her face as he deepened each kiss until there was no room for breath or words between them.

When her orgasm took her it was a gentle but all consuming one. She was swallowed by a warm swell of ecstasy until she was mindless to all but the pleasure. Time had no worth or meaning in that place of joy, and she lost all sense of self and consequence. She became light. She became love.

The hot flood of Cinder's come filled her full to bursting, carrying her deeper into climax, into pleasure. His tears salted her mouth as he moaned against her lips, finding his own fulfillment.

His hips rocked gently in the cradle of hers, pumping every last bit of his release deep into her body. And as she came down from her endless time spent in the heavens she became aware of hands that were not hers or Cinder's cupping her head. She looked down at the mirror that graced the wall beyond the foot of the bed and saw a dark, cloaked form towering over them. She gasped and froze as she became aware of the man that stood over their head, watching and guarding them in silence. She cried out in surprise, but choked on it as her breath froze to ice in her lungs.

She couldn't breathe.

Cinder left her body and the cold spread from her lungs and on through her limbs. It consumed her. Swallowed her up completely. Until there was nothing but icy blackness waiting to claim her.

"Hold on, Steffy. Please just breathe. Breathe." She heard Cinder's voice but it seemed so far away to her now.

Another voice was taking her deep, riding with her the cold that raced through her veins.

"Stay with us, Steffy. Stay. Stay…"

Black eyes, deep and fathomless and filled with the shine of silver stars, flooded her vision. Endless eyes. Ageless.

"It's cold," she heard herself say in a whisper and knew that she was dying at last.

But would she live beyond that death? Would she cross that threshold and become something other than human? She heard Cinder cry out something but the words were lost in the ceaseless murmuring command of that other's voice. And she knew that it didn't matter what happened after…so long as she *lived.*

A flash of light blinded her. A doorway lay open before her, a doorway leading to a void in which pain and suffering and *feeling* were all but memories. She knew that if she stepped over the threshold of that doorway then she would never have to worry about anything ever again. It was calm and tranquil beyond that door.

Beyond that door lay death. And all of its eternal trappings.

The cold that permeated her body beat at her with the sting of a thousand icy knives. If she crossed through the doorway ahead that pain would leave. She knew it. And it would be so easy to let go.

The doorway loomed.

She moved to step through it. But something blocked her path. It was a woman, blonde and tall and lovely despite her crooked nose. A broken nose that Steffy knew the woman had received in a mock fight with her older tomboy of a sister.

"Raine."

"Go back, Steffy. You must go back." Her voice held just an echo of its former radiance.

"Oh Raine. I've missed you so much."

"I know." The woman's smile was sad but full of the warm light of true and loving friendship. "I've been with you. And you've been with me in my dark place. I'll always be with you, Steffy. But you must go back now. I won't let you pass."

"*Steffy*." The Traveler's voice called to her over the distance. He was at her back, coming after her.

"Go on, stupid. You don't want to be here. Go back to your man." Raine sounded so much like her old self that Steffy felt tears fall on her face.

"I love you, Raine," she cried even as she turned back away from the light, into darkness. She hoped her friend heard, but was too far gone to wait around and find out.

Everything went black. Pain and heat engulfed her, welcoming her back to life. She opened her eyes to see Obsidian, Agate, and The Traveler looming over her, healing and protecting her broken body. She looked around for Cinder and winced at the bombardment of striking images that assailed her.

Seeing through a Shikar's eyes was like nothing she could have imagined.

At once she felt Cinder's hand, hot and strong in hers. And knew that she would never have to let it go if she didn't want to.

And she never would.

Chapter Seventeen

"How can you concentrate with all that infernal racket going on?" Edge roared over the music blaring from her stereo.

Steffy glared at him across the practice room and stuck her tongue out at him. She liked Edge, found him rather amusing at times despite his determined seriousness, but learning the foils under his tutelage was no picnic, or so she was discovering. "It helps me keep my rhythm."

"By Grimm, but it's giving me a pounding headache."

"Get over it, you big baby. It's not my fault you have absolutely no taste in music."

"Let's run through the routine once more and call it a day. I can't take much more of this."

Steffy and Edge faced off on opposite sides of the massive room. Steffy clenched her fists, flexed her muscles and felt the tingling of her foils as they shifted beneath her skin, deep within her Shikar bones. She braced her legs apart in a fighting stance and let the pounding rhythm of the music take her.

Weapon of Choice by Fat Boy Slim. How apropos for the moment, she thought with a grin. A simple flexing of her muscles and two long, sickle-shaped blades extended out of the top of her wrists, curving wickedly over her fists. She did so love the look of her blades like this.

Over the course of the past month she'd become a formidable member of the Foil Caste.

Poor Cinder had been so disappointed that she hadn't shown Incinerator abilities as Cady had. He'd mistakenly assumed that all humans crossed over into Incinerator status when they left their humanity behind. She'd had to console him out of his black mood by wrapping her lips around his cock and sucking him dry.

Ahh, the duties of a Shikar wife were never done.

"Come at me, Steffy." Edge's voice interrupted her thoughts.

She felt the silly, lovesick grin she wore and immediately pursed her lips against it. The music beat at her and she lunged at her sparring partner with deadly intent.

Their blades met and sparked. Edge danced with endless speed and grace, motions so fast they blurred. Steffy followed suit, trying to match him move for move. It was difficult, but she held her own. They danced their deadly reel, twirling and lunging and retreating as the music played about them.

Steffy whirled and threw one of her foils at Edge with wicked precision. Edge halted in mid lunge, executed a stunningly dramatic back flip, and just barely avoided being sliced by the silvery-blue blade. The blade boomeranged and Edge kicked out at it with a long blade that shot out of the tip of his booted foot, splitting the sole of the boot wide as he did so.

No wonder the Shikar seamstresses were always complaining of their endless workload.

The blade ricocheted and flew at Steffy's head. She held out her arm—the one that had originally thrown the blade—and tried not to wince as she waited. The foil returned to its mistress, settling into her arm with surprisingly painless ease.

"Quit flinching, woman! How many times do I have to tell you? The blades will return to you without injuring you. You cannot be harmed by your own foils," he admonished her.

"Sorry," she wailed for what was probably the hundredth time. "I can't help it." She danced a jig in time with the music, loosening up her tired muscles as best she could through the exercise.

"Can we please turn off that damn noise?"

"No. I need it." Steffy had grown fond of torturing her teacher over the past few weeks. He was so funny to her when he was riled. It went against the slick, elegant exterior he wore like a shield.

Edge's black trench coat fluttered about his ruined boot with his volatile movements.

"Did you ask if Agate was finished with my trench coat when you saw her earlier?" she asked, eyeing his coat with a lustful eye. Damn but she loved his coat. And she couldn't wait to get her own.

"No. I was too busy getting my own clothing order filled."

"Good grief. How many changes of clothes do you go through anyway?" she asked, noting the foil-sliced tatters of his black clothing.

"I used to only need new boots or coats."

"What do you mean?"

"Before I began training you I used to fight in the nude under my coat. But Cinder will have none of that. He threatened to barby-Q me if I so much as left my arms bare in front of you," he said testily. "Whatever the hell barby-Q means. No doubt something only an Incinerator would understand."

Steffy roared with laughter. "In the nude? I don't believe it—*you*? The staid and serious Edge? Oh that's too precious." She guffawed.

"I can assure you that 'precious' would be the last word in your mind if you were to see me nude," he said blackly, eyes glittering dangerously in the face of her mirth.

"But we'll never know that will we, Edge?"

Cinder's voice never ceased to send pools of liquid hot desire flooding between her thighs.

Steffy grinned at her mate and launched herself into his arms. Cinder's heat enveloped her as he swung her up in his arms and clutched her tight.

His eyes blazed a warning over her at Edge.

Edge rolled his eyes and held his hands up. "Don't get bent out of shape. You can have her—and her damned music. I'll save my charms for a more worthy partner. In fact, a worthy partner awaits me in Egypt as we speak. So if you'll excuse me—"

"Not just now, Edge, I'm afraid. Tryton wants you in his chambers posthaste."

Edge immediately sobered. "What about?"

"I didn't ask."

Without further words wasted between them, Edge left to meet with Tryton.

"Alone at last," Cinder said and kissed her soundly on the lips.

"Not here. Anyone could come by and see."

"So? Let them look. Maybe they'll learn something new."

"You're crazy," she laughed.

"Will you be happy here with a crazy Shikar for your mate?"

She smiled. "Of course I will. I expect you'll see to it."

"Do you mind giving up your life above?" Though his words were serious, his hands played teasingly over her body as he held her close.

"I'll still be working Friday nights at the club, at least for a little while, so I won't be giving up everything all at once."

"I still don't like the idea of you working—even if it's only for one night every week."

"Poor baby. But you'll be with me to make sure I don't get into any trouble."

"You'd better believe it." He smiled wickedly then, and a burning red foil shot out of one of his fingertips, cutting a scorching line through the shirt she wore. It fell away from her in the next breath and she gasped. "Remember last night when I introduced you to the *Smyl*?"

How could she forget that incredible experience? She nodded, feeling her excitement rise until she was practically giddy with it.

"Well I didn't bring a *Smyl*. But I did bring something else." He retrieved a set of small, round, iridescent patches.

"What are those?"

He reached out and popped her breasts free of the bra that encased them. Her nipples immediately peaked as his eyes burned over her. He placed the patches over her nipples, fingers playing her teasingly as he did so. The patches, feeling like wet, hot mouths sucked and pulled and bit at her nipples—so sensuous and erotic that she was immediately in thrall to a burning hot desire.

"*Scheiße*!"

"Mmm. *Scheiße*, indeed. And while those *Nippers* suck and lick your luscious nipples, my mouth will suck and lick your luscious pussy." He bent before her, taking her pants to her ankles as he did so.

"Lay down and put your ankles around my neck," he commanded wickedly.

"Oh my," she said unsteadily and moved to do as he instructed.

His mouth settled without further preamble on the flesh of her cunt. He burrowed his face deep against her, using his tongue like a cock to fuck her with. His fingers entered her along with that tongue, gathering her wetness before it moved down and gently, slowly pierced her anus. Steffy moaned and bucked against him.

His teeth clicked repeatedly against her labia ring. The *Nippers* sucked her nipples until they were hard, pouting, aching. Her breasts bounced as she rode her husband's face and her breath came in sobbing pants. Her fingers clutched desperately in his hair, seeking an anchor in the storm that swept over her and through her.

His finger thrust deeper into her ass, stroking some secret, magical place inside her with expert ease.

"*Scheiße*!" she cried again.

"Scream for me, Steffy. I won't stop until you scream this time," he growled into the mound of her pussy.

Steffy looked down and saw his eyes blazing their Shikar fire over his mouthful of wet sex. His mouthful of her sex.

"Make me," she goaded with a smile, grinding her pussy against his face with shameless abandon.

His slurped her clit noisily into his mouth. He bit and sucked her until she swelled and trembled against him.

"Fuck," she gasped.

"I'm trying to," he said around her clit.

His finger thrust and thrust and thrust again. His tongue licked her over and over, drinking in her wetness. His lips pressed and nibbled against her mercilessly.

Just when she thought she would break, when she thought she would come, he pulled back.

"Not yet. You haven't screamed for me yet."

"Oh my god," she wailed, knowing she was in for it now.

He sat back on his heels, jerked her roughly to him and grinned a devil's grin. Steffy moaned. He lifted her up until only her shoulders, neck and head touched the floor. She was nearly standing on her head. With easy strength he pulled her hips up to his mouth and began licking her like she was an ice cream or lollipop.

She wrapped her legs around his neck and held on for dear life.

He rooted against her, moving his face back and forth against her like a dog with a bone. The enthusiastic movement shocked Steffy into a cry, even as his tongue delved deep into her channel. He filled her with his tongue, licking her deep inside with it. He tasted the very heart of her with an endless, insatiable hunger.

Heat filled her, his power flowing into her unchecked.

She gritted her teeth against a scream.

The *Nippers* pulled on her nipples until she almost came.

Cinder anchored her against him with an arm around her waist. He removed his tongue and thrust three long fingers into the depths of her. He moved down…he wouldn't…

He did.

He buried his face between the cheeks of her ass and speared his tongue into her.

Steffy exploded.

Her scream echoed through the halls of the underground Shikar city.

* * * * *

Grimm smiled to himself as Steffy's cry intruded into his brooding thoughts. He was glad to have another human join their ranks. But his smile faded as quickly as it had come. Darker things than Steffy and Cinder's pleasure occupied him now.

He'd *seen* her.

There had been a moment when he'd seen the flash of her face in Steffy's mind as he'd held her soul anchored to her physical form. It had shocked him, confused him. Then, when she had escaped his grasp and he'd followed her into the realm beyond…he'd seen her again. Steffy had *known* her.

His golden-haired Venus. The woman who had occupied his thoughts incessantly since he'd first seen her that long ago night when he'd saved Cady from her human death. The woman who he'd also saved—or so he thought—sending her back to the living world from which she'd strayed.

Had she died then or later, after he'd sent her back?

He couldn't bear it, this pain. He'd only been able to endure his increasing loneliness these past few years by cradling the knowledge to him that this woman was out there somewhere. That, perhaps, after his duty to Tryton and his people had been fulfilled he might have a chance to find her. To be with her.

But now such a thing was impossible. She dwelled in the land beyond now, which meant she was well and truly gone from him. He could try and hunt her down in that realm—it was not beyond his power to do such a thing—but he doubted even he could succeed in such a fool's quest.

She was lost to him now.

He gritted his teeth against the pain of that loss. Well…it was foolish of him to entertain such fantasies in the first place, he supposed. He was not the type of man who could so easily let go his ties to his people and duty over—of all things—a human woman.

He pulled the black cowl farther over his face and wondered ironically if he wore the shadowy covering to hide away from others, or from himself.

The fire in the grate before him blazed in a roar and Tryton's form appeared, a nebulous shape in the flames.

His leader called him. Duty called him. And it was just as well, really.

Duty was all he had left now.

Epilogue

"It is done. You will accompany Edge to Paris tonight and seek out any Daemon sign. After that you will move on to Ontario and then on to New York. My scouts have reported signs of the Horde's presence in each of these places," Tryton said with a great sigh of weary acceptance.

"What about the others?"

"Steffy is still learning her craft. She cannot fight with us yet, so I'll have Cinder run patrol at the Gates so that he can stay closer to her side. Cady and Obsidian will scout out San Francisco, Tokyo, and Kathmandu, where other Daemon sightings have been reported."

"The tide is turning."

"Yes, but which way? For centuries we have been at a stalemate with the Horde. But now we are at last in open war with them and I do not know for certain who will be the victor."

"Would I not better serve our people by continuing my search for the leader of the Horde army?" He broached the subject that he knew brought the most pain to his friend and leader. But he could not go on this new mission without once more offering his services in finding the Horde's ruler.

Daemon. The Lord of the Horde, himself.

Tryton sighed. "No, old friend. You have spent too many long years looking for him already. He will never be found. I'm not sure he even exists after so many years in the shadows. We must meet this threat head on. I must send you out into the Territories."

"As you wish."

"If you encounter any Daemons you are to report back here with all haste. The monsters are growing too cunning, too strong. I will not endanger you or any of my warriors by leaving you to fight with so small a number. If and when you come across members of the Horde you will come here for reinforcements."

"As you wish," he repeated.

Tryton stared into the shadows of his room, brooding. Grimm joined him in silence, knowing his friend needed what comfort his company could give. "We no longer search for backdoors. To think there was such a time when we cowered with the knowledge that the Daemons could enter the world in such a way, through portals in the Earth." Tryton laughed but the sound was devoid of any mirth or warmth. "Now we search for signs of Traveling Daemons in the Territories. How did it come to this?"

"It was only a matter of time before the Horde moved against us. Against the people of Earth. You knew they would not be content to stay trapped within their borders forever."

"I remember a time when there were no monsters. No Horde army."

"It was a simpler time. But simple times do not last," Grimm murmured. "Everything progresses. Everything grows more complex as the years pass by."

"I hate progress," Tryton said and his tone was almost petulant. It was a surprising emotion from so staid and respected a man.

Grimm nodded. "And that is why we are here. Hiding away from the world which used to be ours just as much as it is now the humans'."

"But progress found us. The world moves and we move with it."

"It is ever the way of things."

"You are a comfort to me, my old friend."

A flash of golden hair and cornflower blue eyes burned into Grimm's mind. "And you are a comfort to me as well, Tryton," he said hoarsely.

"Look at us. Two old men, brooding over our misfortunes." Tryton forced a smile. "We will see these dark times through, you and I. As we always have done. And we will persevere."

"We will win this war, Tryton. To the last warrior, we will fight until it is done."

"And that, Grimm, is what frightens me the most. For where will we be when the last man is standing? And what will it be worth, our last stand against the Horde? The end of our race. The end of theirs. And for what?"

"For honor, Tryton. And what better reason than that?"

Tryton smiled as he visibly rallied his waning spirits. "What better reason? Indeed there isn't one. Indeed there isn't one, my friend."

Enjoy this excerpt from:

MATING SEASON

MOON LUST III

Ash looked about him at the gathering of werewolves. Tonight was the night of the full moon and here in the village proper all would gather and rejoice in the change, in the transformation from biped to quadruped, from humanoid to wolf. He'd never witnessed the change of any outside his own race, a tribe of skin walkers native to the rain forests of Washington State. The Lukoiwai tribe. This would be his first hunt with people other than his beloved relatives.

Just then a small woman caught his eye. She was somehow different from the others who surrounded her. More slight of build, more delicate in bone structure. She looked quite young, in her late teens perhaps, but then age was often difficult to discern among the members of a shapeshifter pack. Ash couldn't resist giving in to the urge to scent her on the wind. He found her naturally wild and sweet, perfume much to his liking. He moved closer into the throng of people, leaving Brianna behind with her children. He felt a great need to draw closer to this small woman.

There was just *something* about her.

Darkness was falling but it was no deterrent to the vision of his nocturnal eyes. He could clearly see his quarry as he approached. He was behind her now, stalking her, though he tried to pretend it wasn't anything so serious as that.

Oh, but it was. And it was growing all the more serious with each passing breath. He scented her again, taking her deep into his lungs.

The woman turned, startling him out of the near trance in which he'd found himself. Her eyes were violet! A shocking, iridescent and ever-shifting hue, which left him feeling as if he'd just received a kick to his stomach. Her eyes glowed in the dark from beneath a long fringe of lashes. It was difficult to pull his gaze away, but he managed after much effort. It was then that he took in the sight of the rest of her form.

She was indeed small, as he'd originally thought. Now that he stood closer to her he could plainly discern that she stood at least a foot shorter than his own six foot four inches. It was this height perhaps, which had first led him to assume that she was still a child of tender years, but her woman's form attested to the truth that she was anything but a child. Her breasts were full, voluptuous for her slight build. Her waist was tiny—no more than a hand span—her hips full and flaring enough to lend her a classical hourglass figure. Her skin was dewy and fresh, her lips a tender cupid's bow. Her nose was tiny on her oval face, her eyes slanted and large beneath elegant brows. She looked like a Botticelli angel made real and in the flesh.

Her hair was caught up under a worn Siberian lynx fur hat. His fingers itched to free it of its confines, and he actually had to catch himself from moving forward to do so. The woman seemed to sense his impulse and raised an eyebrow arrogantly, as if daring him to try it.

The moon was on the rise. The woman turned away from him, clearly dismissing him entirely from her notice, which nearly maddened Ash. But it was too late to give in to his impulses, which were to grab the woman and drag her off into the shadows of the forest. There came a great howl from the gathered pack, and as one they began their transformation beneath the light of the moon. Ash, being of a different race, was not synchronized with the others. He had just enough time to look across the crowd of wolves to see his cousin, Adrian, lounging against a small building with Brianna and her children.

Ash wondered if his cousin would participate in the group's hunt. Adrian was an alpha male, and in their tribe that gave him the power to deny his change should he choose. He was indeed powerful enough to avoid the transformation for several moons. As a youth, Ash had teased him mercilessly about it—Adrian hadn't begun to change with the moon until he was fifteen years old, several years later than most. He had been a late bloomer. But he was the strongest male their pack had seen in memory, late bloomer or not. He now commanded the respect and devotion of all their brethren.

Whether Adrian wanted it or not.

Ash's pensive thoughts were interrupted as his flesh rippled deliciously. He moaned with the pleasure of his impending transformation. Glossy black fur sprung out all over his body. He quickly divested himself of clothing and willingly—gladly—let nature take its course. Within seconds he was settled on four padded feet, his black pelt thick and full over his wolf form. He felt full and swollen with excited moon lust. He looked up at the moon and howled. Dozens of other wolf voices joined his in exultation, their calls echoing in his sensitive ears. He flexed his new muscles and waited for the signal from the great alpha male that stood poised with his mate at the head of the pack.

A flood of power washed over the group, the power of the alpha Bodark. Thus the signal was given and received. As one the pack launched into motion, spreading out once they reached the shelter of the deep forest, to hunt their prey in the moonlit night. A stag's trail glowed like a beacon before Ash's preternatural eyes and he followed it at once, hot on the trail of the mighty animal. He scented the air, using his every instinct to track it.

An elusive perfume caught at Ash's senses. Sweet and evocative, it aroused him to a fever pitch and he turned from one prey and began to hunt another.

The female. She was in heat! Fertile, ripe and ready for mating.

She was up ahead. Not far at all, really, though she was running through the wood on her four graceful legs. Her silver pelt shone like a star in the moonlight, bright and glossy despite the dimming shadows. He raced after her, panting and eager to capture and cover her, his heart bursting with need and desire...

About the author:

Sherri L. King lives in the American Mid-West with her husband, artist and illustrator Darrell King. Critically acclaimed author of The Horde Wars and Moon Lust series, her primary interests lie in the world of action packed paranormals, though she's been known to dabble in several other genres as time permits.

Sherri welcomes mail from readers. You can write to her c/o Ellora's Cave Publishing at 1337 Commerce Drive, Suite 13, Stow OH 44224.

Also by Sherri L. King:

Available in ebook

Moon Lust *Moon Lust*

Rayven's Awakening *Chronicles of the Aware*

Ravenous *The Horde Wars I*

Icarus—*Midnight Desires anthology*

Bitten *Moon Lust II*

Mating Season *Moon Lust III*

Wanton Fire *The Horde Wars II*

Bachelorette

Razor's Edge *The Horde Wars III*

Fetish

Feral Heat *Moon Lust IV*

Manaconda —Sacred Eden *The Horde Wars IV*

Lord Of The Deep *The Horde Wars V*

The Jewel

Overexposed *Voyeurs I – Ellora's Cavemen Tales from the Temple III anthology*

Available in Print

Primal Heat —Moon Lust *Moon Lust I*

Ravenous *The Horde Wars I*

Fetish

Manaconda —Sacred Eden *The Horde Wars IV*

Overexposed *Voyeurs I – Ellora's Cavemen Tales from the Temple III anthology*

Why an electronic book?

We live in the Information Age—an exciting time in the history of human civilization in which technology rules supreme and continues to progress in leaps and bounds every minute of every hour of every day. For a multitude of reasons, more and more avid literary fans are opting to purchase e-books instead of paperbacks. The question to those not yet initiated to the world of electronic reading is simply: *why?*

1. *Price.* An electronic title at Ellora's Cave Publishing runs anywhere from 40-75% less than the cover price of the exact same title in paperback format. Why? Cold mathematics. It is less expensive to publish an e-book than it is to publish a paperback, so the savings are passed along to the consumer.
2. *Space.* Running out of room to house your paperback books? That is one worry you will never have with electronic novels. For a low one-time cost, you can purchase a handheld computer designed specifically for e-reading purposes. Many e-readers are larger than the average handheld, giving you plenty of screen room. Better yet, hundreds of titles can be stored within your new library—a single microchip. (Please note that Ellora's Cave does not endorse any specific brands. You can check our website at www.ellorascave.com for customer recommendations we make available to new consumers.)

3. *Mobility*. Because your new library now consists of only a microchip, your entire cache of books can be taken with you wherever you go.
4. *Personal preferences are accounted for*. Are the words you are currently reading too small? Too large? Too...**ANNOYING**? Paperback books cannot be modified according to personal preferences, but e-books can.
5. *Innovation*. The way you read a book is not the only advancement the Information Age has gifted the literary community with. There is also the factor of what you can read. Ellora's Cave Publishing will be introducing a new line of interactive titles that are available in e-book format only.
6. *Instant gratification*. Is it the middle of the night and all the bookstores are closed? Are you tired of waiting days—sometimes weeks—for online and offline bookstores to ship the novels you bought? Ellora's Cave Publishing sells instantaneous downloads 24 hours a day, 7 days a week, 365 days a year. Our e-book delivery system is 100% automated, meaning your order is filled as soon as you pay for it.

Those are a few of the top reasons why electronic novels are displacing paperbacks for many an avid reader. As always, Ellora's Cave Publishing welcomes your questions and comments. We invite you to email us at service@ellorascave.com or write to us directly at: 1337 Commerce Drive, Suite 13, Stow OH 44224.

Printed in the United States
82431LV00007B/49-54/A

9 781419 951145